The Eighth Armada Gh

The Eighth Armada Gh

🚢
This Armada book belongs to:

_____

_____

_____

Other Spinechillers in Armada

Armada Ghost Books Nos. 1-15

edited by Christine Bernard and Mary Danby

A Shiver of Spooks
True Ghosts

edited by Christine Bernard

The Monster Trap and Other True Mysteries
The Screaming Skull and Other True Mysteries
The Restless Bones and Other True Mysteries
The Hell Hound and Other True Mysteries
The Vampire Terror and Other True Mysteries

by Peter Haining

Black Harvest

Ann Cheetham

Nightmares

edited by Mary Danby

The Eighth Armada Ghost Book

Edited by Mary Danby

Illustrated by Peter Archer

The Eighth Armada Ghost Book was first
published in the U.K. in 1976 by
Fontana Paperbacks,
8 Grafton Street, London W1X 3LA

This impression 1983

The arrangement of this collection is copyright
© Mary Danby 1976

Printed in Great Britain by
William Collins Sons & Co. Ltd, Glasgow.

CONTENTS

ACKNOWLEDGEMENTS

The editor gratefully acknowledges permission to reprint copyright material to the following:

Rosemary Timperley and Harvey Unna & Stephen Durbridge Ltd. for THE TERRIBLE GAOLER and THE HAUNTED PILLAR-BOX. Both stories copyright © Rosemary Timperley 1976

Roger Malisson for SARAH. Copyright © Roger Malisson 1976

Joyce Marsh for SIR HARRY MORTLAKE'S CLOCK. Copyright © Joyce Marsh 1976

Sydney J. Bounds for DREAM GHOST. Copyright © Sydney J. Bounds 1976

Rick Ferreira and Campbell Thomson & McLaughlin Ltd. for CRUSOE'S PARROT. Copyright © Rick Ferreira 1976

Margot Arnold for THE GIRL IN THE MIRROR. Copyright © Margot Arnold 1976

David Langford for TAKEOVER. Copyright © David Langford 1976

Ruth Cameron and Harvey Unna & Stephen Durbridge Ltd. for A RED, RED ROSE. Copyright © Ruth Cameron 1976

Catherine Gleason for THE WOODSEAVES GHOSTS. Copyright © Catherine Gleason 1976

Charles Thornton for THE HAUNTED RIVER. Copyright © Charles Thornton 1976

TIME AFTER TIME is copyright © Mary Danby 1976

INTRODUCTION

A ghost is sometimes said to be a restless spirit, doomed to wander the earth until it has sorted out some kind of leftover problem. There are ghosts who seek revenge, ghosts who try to right wrongs, and ghosts whose mission is to protect the living. And there are those, of course, who are searching for something, endlessly seeking peace of mind.

Such a phantom is *The Terrible Gaoler*. For years and years he's been looking for his head, although, as Roger points out, it's been there on his shoulders all the time. And *Sarah*, too, is looking for something – vengeance on the employer who worked her to death. But her method of haunting is unusual, to say the least.

There's a mystery to be solved in *Sir Harry Mortlake's Clock*, and who better to let Tony and Gill into the secret than the ghost of Sir Harry himself? Also tying up loose ends is the French lady who meets Jim by *The Haunted Pillar-Box*. She's lost something – something small and really rather gruesome.

When Mandy meets her *Dream Ghost*, she is saved from deadly peril, while Sam is rescued from an unhappy situation by the antics of *Crusoe's Parrot*.

The Girl in the Mirror is a story about two girls who cross the barrier of time. It has an eerie, alarming twist at the end.

Ghost stories are usually about people or animals, but in *Takeover* the haunter is huge and metal, and it's unbeatable at noughts-and-crosses!

When Tom sees a girl throwing *A Red, Red Rose* into Green Pool, he thinks he is dreaming, while the two children who meet *The Woodseaves Ghosts* are offered a fascinating opportunity – to change places and become ghosts themselves.

Brian goes to *The Haunted River* to catch fish, but he's caught up himself in age-old evil, as a terrible scene from the past is re-enacted. And the past echoes across hundreds of years in *Time After Time*, a story which will, I hope, intrigue all of you who have ever been somewhere quite new and thought: "I know this place. I've been here before."

A dozen tales for your chilling delight. If they keep you awake, well, you'll be in good company – with all those other restless spirits!

MARY DANBY

THE TERRIBLE GAOLER

by ROSEMARY TIMPERLEY

HOT. Hot and white. A little white building at the edge of the Moroccan village. Deserted, too. Nothing around it seemed to move, except the four people approaching it: Roger, his father and mother, and the guide, Ahmed.

"What is it?" Roger asked.

"Nothing," said Ahmed, "but once it was a prison, in the bad old colonial days when the French were our masters. Now we have good, up-to-date Moroccan prisons." He said it proudly, as if they were luxury hotels.

Roger liked the way Ahmed spoke of the "bad old days". At home, grown-ups nattered on about the "good old days", making him feel as if he'd missed out on something.

"Can we go inside?" he asked.

"If you wish. It is only a ruin now. Not locked up. Anyone can go in, and come out again. Best sort of prison, no?"

"Depends on your point of view," said Roger's mother. "I don't want to go inside. I'd rather sit under that tree and steam gently. My feet are like burning coals."

"Mine too," said his father, looking from his own shoe-encased feet to Ahmed's sandalled ones, with impertinently curling toes. "You go and look in the prison, if you like, Roger. Your mother and I will sit here in the shade and Ahmed can fill in the gaps in our history."

Roger was off like a shot. Much as he liked Ahmed, he

9

found the guide's potted history lessons a bit much. It was all very well for his parents to enjoy them. They didn't have to have history lessons at school.

"So, I tell you the history of the prison," Ahmed was beginning, like any old schoolteacher, as Roger, with a delicious sense of adventure, made his way alone towards the little white building. The sun burned down on his head. A bit dizzy-making. It was a relief to enter the shadowed doorway of the ruin.

Parts of it really were ruined, with bits of the roof missing, but there were a few scruffy little cells still intact. He looked around hopefully for old bloodstains or mysterious Arabic carvings on the walls; for instruments of torture or even an ancient ball-and-chain. But there was nothing like that. The place, he thought, was a bit like an outside loo without the actual loos. Frankly, it was boring. And so hot. He felt slightly sick with the heat. Indeed, he nearly went straight back to his parents and the guide under the tree, but pride made him stay a little longer.

He sat down on the floor in one of the cells. He'd thought he was quite alone in the place. Then suddenly he saw a large man standing there. He hadn't seen or heard him actually enter. It was unnerving. He got to his feet and backed away a little.

The man was wearing a grey jellabah—that dressing-gown thing that many Arabs wear—and a grey turban was wrapped around his head. Yet he didn't look like an Arab.

"What are you doing here?" he asked Roger. He had a rough voice and a strong cockney accent.

"Only looking round. The guide said I might."

"Where do you come from?"

"London."

"You and me both."

"Are you on holiday, too?" Roger asked politely.

"Nope. Business. I'm looking for my head."

"Your what?" Roger thought he must have misheard.

10

"Head. Head. The thing that should be on my shoulders."

"But it is," said Roger.

"Nah!" The man shook the head he said he hadn't got.

Oh, lor', thought Roger, a nutter. This was a word of which his father, a doctor who specialised in psychiatry, did not approve. All the same, this chap must be a nutter. A nutter who thought he hadn't got a nut. Still, it would be pretty awful to go through life thinking you hadn't got a head, so Roger decided he must be kind. "How do you think you came to lose your head, then?" he asked nicely.

"Lose it? I didn't exactly lose it. It was took. They chopped it off, that's what," said the man.

"Who did?"

"The prisoners. They called me 'The Terrible Gaoler'. They called me a lot of other things too, which I won't besmirch your ears with."

"Besmirch?"

"Dirty. Soil. Make mucky. Bad language makes little boys' ears turn black and drop off, if they hear too much of it." He laughed.

"You mean you were a gaoler here in the bad old colonial days?" Roger asked.

" 'S right. It was my last job. Before that I was a mercenary soldier. That's one who fights for any old side as long as he gets paid. I was with the French occupation force. Then I got a wound which made me unfit to fight, so they gave me this job. I did it so well, though I says it as shouldn't, that they began to send all the worst criminals here. The sort of thieves and murderers who'd stop at nothing. Real, rip-roaring villains. But I was a match for them. I controlled them, all on me tod."

"How?"

"By being villainous back. Chains to keep them still. Beatings to keep them quiet. If they didn't behave, they got no food. They soon behaved. When inspectors came,

11

they were amazed at the nice, quiet little community I founded. None of them ever escaped while I was here. 'Over my dead body,' I used to say. And that was how they all did escape, in the end."

"Over your dead body?" said Roger.

" 'S right, mate."

"But you're *not* dead."

"I am, you know. Dead as a door-nail. Only I'm earth-bound, see? On account of not being able to find my head. And it's a damned sight worse than being egg-bound, which is saying something."

"It must be terrible," said Roger, humouring the man. He added delicately: "I think perhaps you're what my father would call 'disturbed'."

"Your father would be dead right. I'm very disturbed indeed. So would you be if you'd had your head chopped off."

"What exactly happened when they did the chopping?"

"Prison revolt, that's what happened. They must have been plotting it for weeks, the villains. They put some dope in my food—I'll never know how they got hold of it; I wouldn't let them smoke their hashish here, but I expect that's what it was. I passed out. My 'trusty'—Huh! I was a fool to trust him—wasn't chained. Well, I had to have someone to wait on me, didn't I? He took my keys, unlocked the rest, and by the time I came to I was trussed up like a chicken and they were preparing a bonfire, like on Guy Fawkes night, with me as the intended guy."

"Or like Joan of Arc," suggested Roger.

"Not at all like Joan of Arc. She was a holy lady, I was a wicked man."

"Yet you'd been put in charge of criminals, like a good man."

"Good men are no good with criminals. They don't understand them. I did. I didn't blame them for having revenge on me. I'd have done the same in their shoes. Not

12

that they wore any. No, when they'd got me all ready for burning, I said: 'Look, I've only been doing my job. You're on top now and you're going to do me in. Fair enough. But a man about to die should be able to choose how. I don't fancy burning. Too painful. Nor hanging. Too undignified. But beheading—that's what they did to Marie Antoinette and Charles the First. So you be good lads and behead me. You can burn me after, if you like, as I shan't feel nothing then'. That was my request. I didn't understand about death then, you see. I thought it was the end. If I'd known it was going to be like this, neither in one place nor the other—"

"But you're not dead," Roger burst out. "It's all in your mind."

"I don't know what's in my mind! It's in my head and I haven't got my head! Of course I'm dead. All this happened a hundred years ago or more. I've lost count. Do I look like someone a hundred years old?"

"Well—sixty, maybe—"

"Sixty! Are you being funny? Thirty-five. Huh! That shows you're only pretending that I've got a head. If you could really see it, you'd see the young face."

"I'm sorry," said Roger. "Everyone over sixteen looks much the same to me—thirty, forty, sixty. But I'll tell you how we can prove that I can really see your head. Take off your turban and I'll tell you what colour your hair is."

"Waste of time. You're a fibber, or you're mad. You see, they did behead me, as I asked, and after they'd done it, they untied the rest of me and just left me lying there. They started dancing around the fire, like a lot of dervishes, and I got up and walked away—the way a chicken goes on trotting about with its head off. It was only when I was miles away that I realised I'd forgotten to pick up my head and take it with me. I've been haunting this place ever since. I've looked everywhere. It's not fair, you know. Anne got hers back."

13

"Who's Anne?"

"Anne Boleyn. Henry the Eighth's bird. She doesn't wear it, just carries it under her arm."

"And walks the Bloody Tower," agreed Roger.

"None of that swearing! Keep a clean tongue in your head. I'd have had you in chains for that in the good old days."

"Please," said Roger, "let me convince you that you have got your head all right. Let me take your turban off and see your hair. Don't tell me what colour it is. *I'll* tell *you*."

He stretched forward, and the man didn't resist. He felt the turban with his fingers. He wondered what material it was made of, so soft and light it was, like fine ash or cobwebs, with a whiskery, whispery feel against his fingers. He unwound the strange material and revealed the man's hair.

He received quite a shock. He'd expected it to be dark. It wasn't. It was red. Brilliantly red. Bedazzling.

"You have *red* hair," he said quietly. "Very, very red. No one could *imagine* such hair. *Now* do you believe that you've got a head?"

"Well, blow me down," said the other. "Do you mean I've been looking for my head all these years and it's been on my shoulders all the time?"

Roger nodded happily, feeling, he imagined, rather as his father must feel when he'd finally cured a patient of some miserable delusion.

"You've got a head with lots of red hair on it, *and* you're not dead. You can believe that too now, can't you? I think myself that you're not the Terrible Gaoler at all. You're a person who's been reading bits of history and sitting in the sun too long, and it's all got sort of mixed up. Come and meet my parents. My father's a doctor. He'll help you far more than I can—although I've made a start.

14

He unwound the strange material . . .

Fancy you thinking you were beheaded and deaded! You almost had me believing you sometimes!"

"It's a rum do," admitted the man.

"Come and meet my father. Follow me."

Roger went ahead. The man began to follow. Roger walked away from the prison, then looked behind and saw that his "patient" was not following any more. He was returning to the prison, his great big back view with its flame of red hair somehow pathetic and beaten, as if he *had* to stay where he was, even when he didn't want to.

Roger was about to call, then stopped. For he had noticed something strange. Something so very strange that his heart raced with fear, and he turned and ran across to his parents at top speed. Suddenly he didn't understand anything any more.

"Hello, darling," his mother greeted him lightly. "Are you running away from the Terrible Gaoler?"

He stared at her.

She went on: "You should have stayed for Ahmed's history lesson. It was just your bucket of blood. Ahmed has been telling us about the 'bad old days', when the Terrible Gaoler controlled that prison. He was an Englishman, a giant with red hair, who terrorised the prisoners until they rose up against him, went berserk, beheaded him, and were going to burn him—but his body mysteriously vanished without trace, all but the head."

"The body did not vanish," Ahmed said darkly. "It walked away. It is walking still. It haunts the prison, seeking the lost head. But the Terrible Gaoler will never find his head because they burned it on their bonfire until there was nothing left but the finest ash."

Roger stood perfectly still, the heat of the sun reaching down to him like flames of an inverted bonfire. He remembered the fine-ash feeling of that grey turban . . .

"Darling, what's the matter?" His mother's voice, fading into distance. He blacked out.

He came to in his hotel bedroom, his father hovering around.

"What happened?" he whispered.

"A touch of the sun. My fault. I should have watched and warned. Some doctor I am!"

"It wasn't only the sun," said Roger, remembering now. "It was the Terrible Gaoler. I met him in the prison. I thought he was a man who was mentally sick. I was bringing him to you, but he wouldn't come. He couldn't, of course. He's bound to that place, looking for his head. Yet I did get him to believe that his head was there, on his shoulders. It must have been a spirit head, still the same, even after it had been burned to ashes. He was a sort of half-and-half person, neither quite dead nor quite alive. Earthbound, he called it, worse than being egg-bound—"

"Quietly now, old boy. Drink this and go back to sleep," said his father, not believing a word of his story.

His mother had come in. "What was Roger saying about being egg-bound? We haven't eaten any eggs lately."

"He's a bit delirious, poor old lad," said his father.

"He was ever so strict," Roger went on dreamily. "When I mentioned the Bloody Tower, he said he'd have had me in chains for using that word, in the 'good old days'. Ahmed's 'bad old days' were his 'good old days'."

"Who's he talking about?" his mother asked his father.

"He thinks he met someone in the prison. He didn't, of course."

Having swallowed his medicine, Roger began to drift off to sleep. He had a swift, dreamlike image of the Terrible Gaoler, tiny and complete, pictured on the dark background of the lining of his eyelids. And the image turned into a proper dream, in which the Terrible Gaoler said: "I couldn't come and meet your parents, lad. They'd have seen through me. I feel ever so much better, since

17

seeing you. It *is* all in the mind. I'll never be quite normal, so I'll stay in the little white prison. It's home. And now I know I've got my head on my shoulders, I can relax. I'm sorry I frightened you when you left. I shouldn't have let you see me in the sun."

Roger remembered this dream when he awoke. He didn't really understand it, except for the apology at the end. For what had frightened him so terribly when he saw his "patient" returning to the prison was the shadow which the half-and-half-world man had cast on the white wall.

It had been the shadow of a man without a head.

SARAH

by ROGER MALISSON

MICHAEL DEAN was not impressed by his first view of Lawnside House. His father echoed his feelings as they got out of the car.

"Gloomy-looking old dump, isn't it."

"Never mind, John. You'll soon make it fit to live in," said Mrs. Dean, opening the creaky garden gate. "Won't he, Michael?"

"I suppose so," answered Michael doubtfully.

The house was a hundred-year-old mansion that his father was buying. He was a builder and he renovated old houses, converting the rooms into self-contained flats. Michael knew that he was going to have quite a job with this one, because Lawnside House had not been lived in for forty-five years.

"Good heavens!" Mrs. Dean stopped abruptly half way down the path. "What was that?"

A white face had appeared fleetingly at one of the curtained windows, then vanished.

"Oh, don't worry," Michael's father said. "That'll be Miss Heseldine, the owner. I haven't met her yet, but she told the solicitors that she would be here to meet us today. She's very anxious to sell."

"That figures," remarked Michael. Who on earth would want to live in a really tumbledown, decaying old building like this?

The door was open and the Dean family walked straight in. The house smelt musty and old. They found their way

19

to the drawing-room, where Miss Heseldine was waiting to greet them.

"Please sit down, Mr. and Mrs. Dean, and, er—"

"Michael," said Michael.

"Hm. I'm very pleased you have decided to buy," she said with a thin smile, turning straight back to his parents. "I have a private income, but with inflation and so forth I shall be glad of the extra money."

"Yes, of course," said Mr. Dean politely. "I signed the final papers at the solicitors' this morning."

The talk turned to legal matters and Michael, bored, inspected the room. Like the hallway, it was furnished with old-fashioned pieces, and the faded flowered wallpaper was peeling. It was, however, spotlessly clean.

"May I take my wife to see the upstairs rooms, Miss Heseldine?" his father asked.

"Certainly," the old lady replied. "You will forgive me if I stay here. My doctor had advised me to climb as few stairs as possible."

His parents stood up. Michael cast an appealing glance at his mother, but she said:

"You stay here, Michael, and keep Miss Heseldine company. Plenty of time for you to explore later."

And so he was left alone in the chilly room with the chill old woman.

"You don't live here, then, Miss Heseldine?" he asked, when she showed no signs of speaking.

"No," she answered shortly, and that was the end of that little conversation.

From the start, he had not liked Miss Heseldine. She sat stiffly in her high-backed chair, plump and wrinkled, and looked at him with hard eyes. Very like a strict teacher he had once disliked in primary school, thought Michael. He tried to think of something to say.

"It's a very old house," he ventured at last. "Does it have any legends of ghosts?"

The effect on Miss Heseldine was startling.

"Of course not!" she snapped. "What a silly thing to say. What a foolish idea!" And she settled firmly back into her chair, turning towards the fireplace. Michael noticed that her spidery hands were suddenly fidgety, and she kept glancing nervously around the room. After that he gave up trying to talk to her and waited for his parents to come back.

"We shall be staying here on holiday for a few weeks while my husband starts work on the house, Miss Heseldine," Michael's mother told the old lady when they finally came downstairs.

"I am sure you will enjoy it. Raynforth is very popular in the summer," she replied.

"It has a smashing beach," Michael chimed in. "Do you live in the village, Miss Heseldine?"

Miss Heseldine gave him a frosty stare, and for a minute he thought she was going to say something corny, like "Children should be seen and not heard", but she merely said:

"No, I do not. I value my privacy, Mr. Dean," she explained to his father, "and I trust you will contact me, if necessary, only through my solicitors."

"Very well. And now we must be going." Mr. Dean stood up. "May we give you a lift anywhere?"

"Yes, please, as far as the village."

"By the way," said Mrs. Dean warmly as the old woman was getting out of the car, "it was very good of you to have the house tidied and cleaned for us. You really shouldn't have bothered."

For some reason the remark seemed to startle and unnerve Miss Heseldine.

"It was no trouble, Mrs. Dean," she answered shortly.

The Deans went home for three weeks, and during that time the builders painted the outside of the house and lit

21

huge coal fires inside to drive out the damp. Lawnside House looked much more inviting the second time Michael saw it.

Their first few days were spent in organising everything and making friends. Downstairs they only used the kitchen, and on the second floor they lived in three rooms: two bedrooms and one they used for a sitting-cum-dining room. In this way they were able to avoid most of the dust, hammering and debris when the builders, joiners and decorators arrived to convert the rest of the house into flats.

Michael helped his father to shift most of the furniture upstairs into the attics where, his father said, the servants of the house used to sleep in days gone by. He had been looking forward to exploring the attics, but there was nothing of interest. The little rooms were poky and cold with slanting ceilings, and he was glad to return to their cheerful sitting-room.

Michael soon made friends with a group of boys and girls from Raynforth, and began to enjoy his holiday. Raynforth, on the North Yorkshire coast, was partly a fishing village and partly a holiday resort. Michael went swimming or fishing every day, and sometimes walked over to the little town of Limeside with his friends for a game of football with the local team, or to go to the cinema. The weather was glorious that summer, and the five-mile walk took them over some wild and beautiful moorland.

It was one of the best holidays the family had ever had, though Mr. Dean spent the mornings working on the house with the builders and Mrs. Dean sometimes grumbled good-naturedly over having to do the cooking. The first few days flew by and it wasn't until the second week that Michael noticed that there was something extremely odd about Lawnside House.

As first it all seemed so silly and unimportant that he

decided not to tell his parents about it, and they were too busy and happy to notice anything. In fact, Michael only realised what was happening because one day he lost his shoes.

He had been crab-hunting in the rock pools on the beach north of Raynforth with Rob and Janet from the village. They did not see any crabs, but the expedition was fun and they decided to go again the next day. But when Michael went to put on his beach sandals he could not find them, though he distinctly remembered having dropped them, sand-caked and stained, in the corner of his bedroom. After a search, he found them cleaned and polished and neatly placed in his wardrobe. Michael was puzzled. He asked his mother, then his father, if they had touched the shoes, but neither of them had.

After that, he began to notice odd little things. He happened to be an extremely untidy boy, but in the mornings his clothes were always folded away, and if he left books lying around they were always put back into the bookcase; in fact, his room was unusually tidy. Surely he wasn't sleepwalking, and tidying up as he went? That was a ridiculous idea.

One day he decided on an experiment. Rob and Janet came round for supper and a game of Monopoly afterwards. When Michael went to bed he purposely left the board, with its houses, counters, cards and money, scattered about the floor of his room. The next morning the whole game was tucked away into its box.

It was all very strange. He was quite sure that neither of his parents came into his room during the night, and there was no one else in the house. Or was there? He suddenly remembered how anxious and nervous Miss Heseldine had looked when he had jokingly asked her if Lawnside House was haunted. Michael half-believed in ghosts, but he had always understood that they were meant to frighten. He had heard of some, what were they called?

—poltergeists, that was it—which threw the furniture around and made houses tremble. On the other hand, he had never heard of ghosts going about tidying everything away. But what other explanation could there be?

Michael decided to find the answer once and for all. That evening he planned to stay awake all night to see what was going on.

Staying awake was going to be a big problem, of course. That afternoon he had been playing football and he was tired. He read adventure stories with great determination until half past eleven, when he found himself beginning to doze over the page. Midnight was supposed to be the hour that ghosts showed up, wasn't it? Very well, he could easily stay awake for another half hour. Switching off the light, he waited for his eyes to become used to the gloom. It was a fine, moonlit night, and he could make out all the furniture in his room quite well.

Michael straightened himself on the pillow. His head kept falling on to his chest and his eyelids drooped heavily. He tried pinching his fingers to stay awake, but his drowsiness increased. Glancing at the luminous dial of the travelling alarm beside his bed he saw that it was ten to twelve. Ten minutes to go, then. If nothing happened at midnight he would give up and go to sleep.

Two minutes to twelve. Was the room growing colder, or was he imagining that it was? Michael shivered and pulled his dressing-gown tighter round his shoulders. He yawned, and decided that nothing was going to appear. But just as he was snuggling down into bed the handle of the door slowly began to turn. Something or someone was trying to get in . . .

Heart thumping, Michael drew the covers up to his chin, and the hair prickled at the back of his neck as the door opened, inch by inch, without a sound. When it was half open he was astonished to see, not some horrible shrouded creature, but his own football boots floating into the room.

24

They stopped in mid-air and the door closed quietly. He watched breathlessly, his amazement nearly greater than his fright. The boots looked so funny, dangling there in a rather pathetic way, that he almost wanted to laugh. Almost, but not quite, for a frightening thought struck him. Was there some invisible thing in the room with him, holding the boots in its insubstantial hand?

"Who . . . who's there?" he called, trying to keep his voice steady.

He was answered by a despairing wail, and a girl's voice said indignantly, "Oh, it's too bad! You're awake! I simply can't go on—it's all too much!" And then came the sound of sobbing. With a thump, the boots fell to the floor.

Michael cleared his throat. "Er . . . please don't cry," he said awkwardly.

"It's all right for you," said the little voice. "I just can't cope any more, that's all. Painters and decorators! All the rubble! Every night it gets worse. I simply don't know what to tidy first! And the cleaning!"

The voice grumbled on in this strain for several minutes, and Michael grew more puzzled than afraid.

"But who are you?" he asked at last. "Can't I help?"

"Oh, I forgot, you can't see me. There!"

Before his astonished eyes a girl appeared. She was not much older than Michael, but very small and extremely thin. She was dressed in a long grey frock with a white apron and cap. In one hand she held a large, old-fashioned dustpan and brush. For a moment they looked at each other, and then the girl began to laugh.

"Excuse me," she said, "but you looked so funny—so surprised. Your eyes nearly popping!"

"Well, I've never seen a ghost before," Michael pointed out, a little sulkily. He didn't feel afraid of this ghost any more, but he certainly didn't want it—her?—to laugh at him. "Anyhow, you're not my idea of a ghost at all. Shouldn't you be rattling chains and groaning a bit?"

"Oh, no. All I have to do is to tidy up and dust and clean—housework, you know. And as to my not looking like a ghost—feel my hand!"

Michael tried, but his hand closed on cold, empty air.

"Gosh," he said feebly. The experience shocked him rather.

"My name is Sarah," said the girl. "And yours is Michael, of course. I can't get on with my work until you're asleep. You're not supposed to see me, you know."

"But why do you have to do all this housework?" he asked curiously.

"I used to work for Miss Heseldine," explained Sarah, perching on the end of the bed. "I was never strong, and I couldn't do my work very fast. Miss Heseldine is a stickler, you know, and she insisted on having the house spotless all of the time. So I had to work very hard, even when I was ill. Drudge, drudge, all day from morning to night. She had never had a day's illness in her miserable life, so she didn't understand. Would you believe it," said Sarah, warming to her subject, "if she found one speck of dust anywhere she used to send me to bed without any supper. So, anyhow, I worked harder and harder and got weaker and weaker, and in the end I died."

"The inhuman old thing!" cried Michael indignantly. "That's really shocking. You don't seem too upset about it, though," he added.

"Oh, it was nearly fifty years ago now," said Sarah, swinging her legs nonchalantly. "Forgive and forget. Do you happen to know where she's living now?" she enquired, a shade too carelessly.

"No, I'm afraid not . . . why?" asked Michael, suddenly suspicious.

"Well, I wouldn't mind seeing her again, that's all," said Sarah, and her eyes narrowed. "I have a score to settle with her, you see. Only she won't stay here because she knows that I'm around, and I can never find out where she's gone."

Perhaps that's just as well, thought Michael, startled at the crafty look which had crossed her face.

"I'm afraid I've no idea where she is," he told her. "At the seaside she said, but that could be anywhere."

"Never mind, I shall find her one day. Well, I can't stay here chatting all night, I really must get on. Goodnight!"

Sarah vanished, and seconds later Michael was asleep.

As usual, when Michael woke up the next morning, his room was spick and span. He set out for an early morning walk to think about his meeting with the strange little ghost. Glancing back to Lawnside House he shivered slightly. Sarah meant them no harm, he was sure, but it was no wonder that Miss Heseldine had seemed so ill at ease in the house. Once she had realised, more than forty years ago, that her stubborn little servant girl had come back to haunt her, she must have been terrified for her life.

She really ought to have told his father, though, before she had sold him the house. Michael wondered whether to tell his parents about Sarah. But what if the little housemaid hadn't been telling the truth? He remembered how sly she had looked when she spoke of her former mistress. Supposing Miss Heseldine was entirely innocent, and had been driven out of her rightful home through Sarah's spite? Perhaps he had better investigate further before he said anything to his parents.

Michael returned to the house, and after breakfast he hung around the kitchen until Mr. Crabtree came in for his morning coffee. Mr. Crabtree was a professional gardener, and Michael's father had employed him to lick their garden into shape. Michael went to talk to him as he was drinking his coffee and puffing at his pipe.

"You've lived in Raynforth a long time, haven't you, Mr. Crabtree?" he asked.

"All of my sixty-eight years, lad," replied the gardener.

"You would know Miss Heseldine, then?"

"Know her! Aye, everyone knew her. There weren't many liked her, though."

"She didn't seem very friendly when we met her," Michael said.

The old man removed his pipe before answering, deliberately, "She's a hard, cold, selfish, grasping woman. Always was. Vindictive, if you crossed her, and a tyrant as well."

"A tyrant?" asked Michael, hoping he was steering Mr. Crabtree in the right direction.

"That's what I said," nodded the old man. "You ought to have seen the way she lorded it over her servants when she lived here. Not many would stay with her long. They couldn't put up with her finicky ways and endless nagging. Jobs were hard to find in those days, but even so, as I say, not many could stand her so long It was over a servant that she left Raynforth, as it happens."

"Really? How was that?" said Michael encouragingly.

"Well, lad, there was one little girl came up from Wiltshire to be a housemaid. She wasn't more'n fifteen, and a frail, sickly little thing. Well, Miss Heseldine took advantage of her because she was young and had no experience —Sarah, I remember her name was. Miss Heseldine literally worked her to death, and though she could see the girl was wasting away she never saw that she had any medical treatment. It was a crying scandal, lad, and they remember it in these parts yet. Some of the neighbours and the servants talked of going to the police, but nothing ever came of it. A couple of days after Sarah died, Miss Heseldine moved out."

"What a terrible thing," said Michael automatically. He felt rather uneasy, not only because Sarah's story had been confirmed, but because the room had gone colder and he felt sure, though he could not tell why, that Sarah was somewhere about and listening to their conversation. It was an uncomfortable sensation, but he did not feel afraid.

"They were the bad old days, lad. We were all glad when Miss Heseldine took off. And I'll bet," he added, chuckling, "that she doesn't get half as much of her own way as she used to. I don't imagine that the staff of that posh Grand Hotel in Limeside like her any more than we—"

"Hush!" cried Michael. "You mustn't say that!"

"What's the matter, lad? I only said that where she's gone to live, at the Grand Hotel, the staff there . . ."

The old man talked on, but the damage was done. For Michael's quick ear had caught a faint, rather spiteful laugh, and the sound of a gleeful "Goodbye!"

The next morning Michael awoke and looked around his bedroom with a puzzled feeling. There was something unusual—ah! that was it! The room was untidy. Nothing had been put away. The little ghost had gone.

He got out of bed and began straightening the room before his mother saw it. In a way, he realised with a sigh, he was going to miss Sarah. And I bet I know where she's gone, he thought uneasily. The Grand Hotel at Limeside. I hope she doesn't cause too much mischief there.

All that day, Michael tried not to think about what Sarah might be up to. But it wasn't till the following morning that the news broke.

Over breakfast, Mr. Dean exclaimed, "Good heavens! Old Miss Heseldine's died. Look, it's here in the paper. 'Hotel Resident Plunges to her Death'."

"Let me see," said Mrs. Dean, and Michael craned over her shoulder to read it too.

The local paper gave a full account of how Miss Heseldine had tripped over a large, old-fashioned dustpan on the stairs, and had died as a result of her fall. The Hotel

Manager denied that the dustpan belonged to the hotel, and said that the accident was something of a mystery.

Sarah never returned to Lawnside House. Three weeks later the Deans left, and during the months that followed Michael often thought about the old mansion and the ghostly housemaid who had tended it for so many years. He wondered, too, what had become of her now that her mistress was dead, and a year later he thought he had the answer.

Driving through Raynforth one wet day on their way to Scotland, the Deans stopped to see Lawnside House, now converted into smart flats, and to have some lunch. Michael went to say hello to Mr. Crabtree and some friends in the village, and on his way back he took a short cut through the local churchyard.

He knew that Miss Heseldine had been alone in the world, and so it came as rather a shock to see her grave, which should have been overgrown with weeds, neatly tended. The grass was trimmed, some flowers were blooming, and the headstone was polished: R.I.P., it said.

Walking back through the peaceful countryside in the quiet drizzle, Michael could not help shuddering as he wondered whether Miss Heseldine really was resting in peace, or whether her implacable little drudge was waiting upon her still, throughout all eternity.

SIR HARRY MORTLAKE'S CLOCK

by JOYCE MARSH

THE low, grey stone building sprawled rather untidily a few yards from the cliff edge. The Rowan family's battered old car had barely come to a halt on the gravel drive when its doors were flung open and the children, Anthony and Gillian, tumbled out, squealing and shouting in excited merriment. This was the moment they had longed for with such impatient eagerness, but now the waiting days were over. The long journey from London to Devon was done and they had finally arrived at Pontepelly House, which was to be their home for the whole of the long school holidays.

Anthony, the elder of the two, led the way as the children raced to the cliff edge, where they flung themselves down on the short, springy turf to gaze at the beach below. A steep flight of steps led down the cliff face to a tiny, sandy cove curving between two long arms of high rocks, which enclosed it so completely that even at low tide the beach could only be reached from the sea or from the cliff top.

The late sun, hanging low over the sea, darkened the yellow sand to a deep, glowing orange. Here and there rock pools glittered with the rosy reflection of the sunset. It was a quiet, secluded playground, promising hours of exploration and delight. Both children were tempted to begin at once, but their father's voice called from the house.

"Tony, Gill, the beach can wait. Come in now and help your mother with the unpacking."

Fortunately the house itself was a rival attraction. Not only was it large and rambling, but it was very old and had a long, interesting history. It had once been a farmhouse, a fact which was evidenced by its sprawling, irregular shape where the outbuildings had, over the years, been altered and incorporated into the main house.

In the eighteenth century, Pontepelly House had been acquired by a certain Sir Harry Mortlake, and it had remained in the Mortlake family until the present day. Unfortunately, the family resources had been severely depleted by high taxation and poor management, and the present Sir Peter Mortlake was forced to lease out his ancestral home to summer visitors.

Tony and Gill's parents had already begun to carry the suitcases inside, and the children followed them through the thick oak door which led directly into a wide, panelled hall. The polished wooden floor gleamed and threw back the reflections of the brasses and pictures lining the walls, but the children's attention was immediately rivetted upon a huge clock which stood against the wall at the foot of the stairs.

The door of the pendulum case was large enough for a man to pass through, and the intricately carved decoration above the brass face reached to the ceiling. The engraved figures on the dial were faded and difficult to read. No sound came from the clock and, although it was late afternoon, the long gilded hands stood at ten minutes to twelve.

A little jumble of luggage stood neglected in the hall as Dick and Marjory Rowan stood gazing up at the monumental clock.

"Gosh, Dad, what's that? Big Ben's little brother?"

"Well, Tony, it's called a great-great-grandfather clock, but I feel more inclined to call it a super great-great-grandfather clock. It's certainly the largest clock I've ever seen inside a house."

"You can say that again."

Tony had planted himself squarely before the clock and was dwarfed by its great size.

"It's not going, though, Dad. Does it want winding?"

"I'm afraid not, young man. That clock stopped nearly two hundred years ago, and it has never gone since—not properly, that is."

All the Rowans turned as they were joined in the hall by a pleasant-faced, middle-aged lady, who had spoken with a slight, but unmistakable, Devonshire accent.

"I am Mrs. Trevellan," the newcomer went on. "I am housekeeper here, and I hope that I shall be able to make your stay at Pontepelly House both happy and comfortable."

The Rowans introduced themselves, but Tony could hardly wait for these introductions to be completed before returning eagerly to the subject of the clock.

"Do you mean to say that this clock is more than two hundred years old, Mrs. Trevellan?"

"Yes, it is indeed. It is known as the Mortlake clock, and is quite famous, I believe. The first Sir Harry Mortlake built it himself in seventeen hundred and something. His hobby was clock-making. He made dozens of them, but this was his masterpiece. It's one of the largest clocks of its kind in the country. If you look carefully, you will see that it is actually built into the wall; that is because of its great size."

The Rowans obediently peered at the back of the clock and saw that it did appear to be part of the wall.

"Once upon a time," Mrs. Trevellan continued, "it is supposed to have been so accurate that it lost only one minute in ten years, but it stopped the night old Sir Harry disappeared and has never gone since, although any number of experts have been down here to examine it."

Tony, who dearly loved a mystery, could barely wait for Mrs. Trevellan to finish speaking before he burst in with his eager question.

"How did Sir Harry disappear? Was he lost at sea or something?"

"No, my dear, nothing as simple as that. According to the old story, Sir Harry went into that parlour over there, and—" She waved her hand in the direction of one of the doors leading off the hall. "The footman served him his brandy, bade him goodnight, locked all the doors and windows and went to bed. That was the last that anyone ever saw of Sir Harry, for next morning it was discovered that his bed had not been slept in and he was nowhere in the house, although all the doors were still bolted from the inside. The whole place was searched and the panelling examined for secret passages, but nothing was found. Everything was exactly as it should be, except that the clock had stopped at ten to twelve and it has never gone since."

"But you said just now that the clock doesn't go *properly*. Does that mean that it still works after a fashion?"

It was Dick's turn to question Mrs. Trevellan, and it was apparent that his interest was almost as great as his son's.

"Well, no. It is a very peculiar thing, but sometimes the clock will start up of its own accord—always at exactly ten to twelve. It keeps perfect time for a day, and then at ten minutes before midnight it stops again."

"Gosh, that *is* odd. Do you think it will start up while we're here?"

" 'Tis not likely, I fancy. It has only happened four or five times in two hundred years, and the last time was long before I was even born."

Tony looked crestfallen, but was still inclined to pursue the subject of the Mortlake clock, until a sudden, sharp exclamation from his mother interrupted him.

"Gill, whatever is the matter? Are you ill?"

34

For the first time they all noticed that Gillian had taken no part in the conversation, and now she was leaning against the wall. Her face, which only a short time ago had been pink and rosy with excitement, was now pale and drawn. Her arms were folded tightly across her chest and she was trembling violently. Her blue eyes, which were nearly always sparkling with gaiety, were flung wide and they seemed dark with fear as she gazed fixedly at the clock looming above her.

"Gill, what is the matter?" Marjory Rowan asked again anxiously.

"I don't know, Mummy, but I don't like it here. I want to go home. I want to go home now. I'm frightened."

The little girl's voice rose to a scream, and the unnaturally dark eyes brimmed over with tears. Immediately the centuries-old mystery of Sir Harry Mortlake's disappearance was driven from their minds as they hastened to comfort and calm the distraught child.

Gill would not, or could not, tell them of what she was afraid, and eventually they assumed that she was overwrought by excitement and the long journey; so she was put to bed, where she fell asleep holding tightly to her mother's hand.

The hot sun hung in a cloudless sky and painted sparkling silvery splashes on the blue-green sea. The children were on the beach, as they had been every day for the past week. Tony, his body already browned by the sun and sea, was endeavouring for the fiftieth time to balance upright on his makeshift wooden surf-board, which was being continually snatched from beneath his feet by the frothing, seething waves.

Gillian, sitting on the hot sand, watched her brother with listless, uninterested eyes. Then Tony temporarily abandoned his strenuous sport and raced across the sand to fling himself down beside his sister.

"The water's lovely today. Aren't you coming in, Gilly?"

"No—and don't call me Gilly."

She snapped back irritably and, at that, Tony's patience was exhausted.

Since her inexplicable outburst on the day they had arrived at Pontepelly House, Gill had not indulged in any more hysterical demands to be taken home. She had, however, been strangely unlike her usual self. Her little face was pale and pinched; she was as quiet as a mouse and crept about nervously as if every corner, every lurking shadow held some fear for her. Like his parents, Tony had hoped that this strange mood would soon pass, but plainly it was not going to, and the time had come for different methods.

He planted himself before his sister and spoke firmly.

"Now look here, Gill, what is the matter with you? You say you aren't ill, and yet you moon around as if you're afraid of your own shadow. Mum and Dad are worried sick about you. They are even talking of packing in the holiday and taking you home. You are making everyone miserable. It's too bad of you."

Suddenly his voice softened and he dropped down on to the sand beside his sister.

"Come on, kid. We've always talked things out—tell me what's the trouble."

"I don't know, Tony. It sounds so silly."

"Never mind how it sounds, Gill. Just tell me."

"Well . . ." She hesitated for a long while and her lips trembled. "When I am in that house I have the oddest feeling, as if there is something that I must do. I don't know what it is, or why, but I can almost hear someone calling to me: 'Gilly . . . Gilly'. It goes on and on running through my head, pleading for help. There you are, it does sound silly, but it frightens me."

She looked at her brother anxiously as if she expected

36

him to laugh at her, but Tony had no inclination to scoff. One look at her woebegone face was enough to convince him that the strange fears she felt at Pontepelly House were very real to her.

"The voice calls you 'Gilly'," he said thoughtfully. "That's odd, because no one calls you that – at least, only once in a blue moon."

She nodded. "It's always the same—'Gilly'. Oh, and there's another thing: sometimes a silly little rhyme keeps popping into my head. I don't know where I read it, or heard it, but it goes . . .

> *My beloved son, O pity me,*
> *For I have naught to bequeath to thee,*
> *Save a hazardous wealth from over the sea."*

Tony looked at his sister very sharply.

"I know where that rhyme comes from—it's engraved around the face of the clock, but you couldn't have read it because the letters are too worn to be seen properly. Mrs Trevellan told me about it. Perhaps she told you, too?"

Gill shook her head vigorously. "No, no one told me. I just hear it—mostly at night, as if someone was whispering it in my ear while I'm asleep. What does it mean, Tony?"

"I don't know. Apparently, when he disappeared, old Sir Henry left no other will except those few words written on the clock face. His son searched in almost every country but could never find the 'hazardous wealth from over the sea', and his father's fortune had disappeared, too, for the son was left penniless."

"Oh, Tony, I'm fed up with Pontepelly House, with old Sir Harry and his horrid clock. I wish we could go home."

Thick tears ran down Gill's cheeks and, despite the hot sun, she began to shiver violently. Tony placed a protective arm about her shoulders as he gazed thoughtfully out at the sparkling sea. When his sister was more calm, he spoke gently. "I don't think going home now is the answer, Gill. It's just running away, and that never solved anything. No, we must find out who or what and why you are being . . . well, haunted—that's the only word I can think of to describe it."

"But I'm frightened," she said in a small voice.

"I know you are, kid, but you have just got to face up to it; find out what you are being asked to do."

"I can't, Tony. I really can't. When I hear something calling me I say my 'time's tables' over and over until it goes away."

"But that's the trouble—it only goes away for a short while. Next time you must answer the voice. I don't mean you should go around shouting 'What do you want?' as if you were batty. Just concentrate your mind and try to find out what the voice wants of you. Will you try?"

She looked at him pathetically, but after a while nodded slowly and a trifle uncertainly.

"Good girl, but whatever happens you are not to go anywhere or do anything until you have told me first— promise?"

She nodded again and her short dark hair bobbed and gleamed in the bright sun. She smiled, and for the first time in days the smile upon her lips was reflected by a soft gleam in her eyes.

"I feel better now."

" 'Course you do. Telling me was half the battle. You have been dotty keeping it to yourself all this time. Now come and have a go on the surf-board. I've taken enough tumbles—it's your turn now."

For the rest of that day everyone noticed, with some relief, that Gill had at last begun to recover some of her usual high spirits. She went off, quite eagerly, to accompany her parents on a 'courtesy visit' to Sir Peter Mortlake, who, unable to afford to live at Pontepelly House, occupied a small cottage in the village.

With the rest of the family out, and Mrs. Trevellan busily engaged in the kitchen, Tony was alone in the vast and rambling old house. Generations of Mortlakes had altered it, added to it, left their mark upon it, and now, in the shadowy silence, even the practical Tony sensed some of the mystery which seemed to lurk in its dim recesses and odd corners.

Rather glumly he gazed up at the monumental time-piece towering above him and peered at the faint, indecipherable letters engraved around the face. With probing fingers he explored the carved moulding, searching for the hidden spring which, Mrs. Trevellan had told him, was the only way to open the door of the pendulum case. He could not find it, and with a faint shrug he abandoned the search, deciding somewhat apprehensively that his frail, frightened little sister was the only one likely to discover the haunting secret of the Mortlakes and their great clock.

Gillian lay in her bed wide-eyed and sleepless. It was a time which, of late, she had come to dread, for she was alone in her room. All around her the silence of the sleeping house was thick and absolute. The dark shadows, criss-crossed by silvery shafts of moonlight, seemed to hover over her, enfolding her and forming a seemingly impenetrable barrier between herself and the comforting presence of the other people in the house.

Suddenly there was a loud rap on the wall, and at the sound the threatening shadows receded a little, for it was a pre-arranged signal; it told her that Tony, in the next room, was still awake and would come running at her call.

It was reassuring to know that her brother was so close at hand. Gill closed her eyes determinedly, resolving that until she fell asleep she would fill her mind with busy thoughts to keep at bay the strange voice with its insidious calling and pleading.

For a while she thought of Sir Peter Mortlake, whom she had visited with her parents that afternoon. From the very first moment, Gill had liked Sir Peter. A fine network of little lines at the corners of his eyes gave his face a jolly expression, but the eyes themselves were dark with a look of deep sadness—which was not surprising, for Sir Peter would soon have to part with Pontepelly House. She had heard him tell her father that all his efforts to keep the house had failed, and before the year was out the old Mortlake home would pass out of the family, probably for ever.

A picture of Sir Peter seemed to form before her; she saw him quite clearly with his greying hair tumbling over his forehead and his old tweed jacket flecked with the little pieces of ash which fell unheeded from his pipe.

Her body felt light and free, as if she were floating, and the mental picture of Sir Peter became blurred over with a bright mist. Then from the centre of this mistiness another figure formed. The face was Sir Peter's—but now the hair was drawn tightly back and the tweed jacket had become an elegant blue coat made of shiny fabric, with frothy white frills at the neck and wrists. Bright blue eyes were fixed upon her with a desperate urgency. The lips moved . . .

"Gilly, Gilly, . . .
        O, pity me,
        For I have naught . . ."

Gill sat up sharply, abruptly cutting off the words which were running through her mind.

"Once two is two, two two's are four . . ." Desperately she pushed out the frightening voice which filled her head. Then she remembered her promise to Tony. The strange dream-like figure had faded now, but, with an effort, she conquered her fear. Closing her eyes again she recalled every detail of the man who, but a moment before, had seemed so real.

"What do you want of me?" She whispered the words into the still darkness.

"Come. I will show you. Be not afraid, Gilly."

The answer was not spoken aloud, but came as if from her own mind.

Suddenly unafraid, Gill left her bed and slipped out on to the landing. The bright moon could not reach in through the high windows, and it was very dark as Gill's bare feet padded across the polished floor to the head of the stairs.

In the hall below a shaft of light struck across the clock face, and it gleamed in the darkness like beaten gold. The great clock glowed with a misty light, shot through with rainbow colours. The colours streamed and blended together until they became a pair of bright blue eyes. Gill looked down into those eyes and read in them the answer —she knew now what she must do.

She remembered her second promise to Tony and, turning quickly, she ran to his room. The boy was not asleep and he sat up as his sister burst into the bedroom.

"Tony, come quickly. I know now what I must do, and there is not much time. What does your watch say?"

Tony opened his mouth to speak, but she cut him off. "Please, no questions now—I must hurry."

Her brother obediently rolled over and consulted his watch. "It's exactly quarter to twelve," he said. "And I know that's right. I checked my watch with the radio."

Gill barely waited for him to finish speaking before she ran out, and the bewildered boy quickly joined her on the landing.

"Come on," she said. "I have to start up the clock— and it must be done at exactly ten to twelve."

41

Tony followed as her small white-clad figure sped down the wide, shallow stairs.

"Hang on a minute, Gill. You don't know *how* to start the clock. You don't know even how to open the case."

She did not bother to answer; she had already reached the clock and her fingers went out unerringly to a carved leaf in the decorative moulding. There was a sharp click and the door of the pendulum case sprang open a few inches. Long years of disuse had stiffened the hinges, and both children pulled hard at the door until, with a loud creak, it opened wide.

Inside the weights were pulled high and the great pendulum hung straight and still.

"Tell me when it's ten to twelve exactly."

Moving slightly so that a patch of moonlight shone upon his watch, Tony carefully counted off the seconds.

"Five, four, three, two, one . . . now!" he said.

Gill's finger barely touched the pendulum before it began to swing, and suddenly the whole house seemed to echo with the deep ticking of the clock.

"That's it," Gill said with a little sigh of satisfaction. "Now there is nothing else to be done for the moment."

Tony was agog with curiosity, but by now Gill's eyes were almost closing with weariness, and he tactfully postponed his questions until the morning.

The next day the household had awakened to the unaccustomed sound of the Mortlake clock as it ticked off the seconds, sending the sound of their passing echoing through the house.

Sir Peter was sent for immediately, and he came posthaste to see his clock, which, as he told them excitedly, had not started up since his great-grandfather's time. From then on the house saw a constant stream of visitors; for it seemed that the entire village must come to see for themselves. Little groups of them gazed up at the clock as it once more measured out the time, and they wondered

42

what strange circumstance had set it going. But the two children who knew the answer held the knowledge to themselves.

Gill had not been able to explain her actions on the night before very satisfactorily.

"It came to me in a sort of dream," was all she could tell her brother. "But you wait until tonight," she added, and it was these words which filled Tony with a sense of nervous apprehension.

The glowing sunset had faded and the purple velvet of the night sky was spangled with a host of tiny stars. The last of the visitors had finally left, and the household slept. All, that is, except Tony. So anxious was he for his sister that he had crept from his own room to sit watching by her bed. She appeared to be sleeping peacefully, but suddenly her eyes flew open and she sat up abruptly.

"It's almost time," she said, without expressing any surprise at finding her brother sitting by her side.

She slipped out of bed, and together the children crossed the landing to the head of the stairs.

Only the ticking of the clock disturbed the silence and, in the moonlight, the hands could be seen standing at a quarter to twelve. Quietly, Gill sat down on the top stair, resting her head against the carved banisters, and Tony dropped down beside her.

Abruptly came the sharp sound of a door opening, cutting across the regular ticking of the clock. Gill turned to her brother and her eyes glittered with excitement. Soundlessly she put a finger to her lips and then pointed down the stairs.

The door of the parlour swung slowly open, a blue radiance streamed out, and then, framed in the doorway, the children saw the bright figure of a man. For a moment he paused there, motionless. He was very tall, with long powdered hair tied into the nape of his neck with a broad black ribbon; the shiny fabric of his blue coat gleamed softly. He yawned slightly and held one pale hand before his mouth in an elegant gesture. From his wrists, white lace hung in a cascade of billowing frills.

Effortlessly, seeming to glide rather than walk, the glowing apparition began to cross the hall. At the foot of the stairs he glanced upwards and his eyes looked straight into Gill's. He seemed to smile, and then one elegant hand reached out to the clock. There was a faint click and the pendulum case sprang open. The hands showed exactly ten to twelve as the figure, still shining with an unnatural brightness, leaned inside and grasped the pendulum.

The ticking stopped and, by contrast, the ensuing silence seemed more absolute. With one last glance up the stairs to where the children were sitting, the man stepped inside the clock and the door slowly closed behind him. The ethereal radiance which had lit the hall faded away, and Gill moved swiftly. She would have sped on down the stairs had not her brother held her back.

"Gill, you can't go down there."

Their positions had been reversed—now it was Tony who was nervous while Gill was confident and excited.

"There's nothing to be afraid of, Tony. That was old Sir Harry Mortlake. He wants me to follow him. He wants me to know where he disappeared to, and that's why he's been calling to me and why he came last night and told me to start up the clock."

"I don't understand."

"Neither do I, exactly, but I know that Sir Harry must have stopped the clock the night he vanished, and he wanted me to start it up again so that everything would be the same as it was that night. Then he could come back and show me—whatever it is he wants to show me or wants me to know."

It was a very involved explanation, but it made some sort of sense. Gill believed so, anyway, for she was already half way downstairs, and by the time Tony had joined her

The glowing apparition began to cross the hall . . .

in the hall she had already swung open the door of the clock. Her slender figure gleamed whitely in the moonlight as she bent forward into the clock. Her fingers quickly found what they sought. There was a sharp sound, then, creaking slightly, the whole back of the clock slid away and the two children found themselves looking into a black, yawning opening. A dank, musty odour wafted out, and far away they could hear a faint rushing sound.

"There you are!" Gill said triumphantly. "That's how Sir Harry Mortlake left the house. And, of course, that's why the clock stopped—for he couldn't pass through the opening while the pendulum was still swinging."

Impulsively, she stepped into the clock case, and would have passed through the opening, but once again Tony held her back.

"Hang on a minute. Just cool it, Gill. I'm going to fetch a torch and something warmer for you to wear, then we can go and find out why Sir Harry Mortlake had a secret passage leading out of his house—and why he went through it and never came back."

Fortunately there was a torch in the cupboard where they hung their outdoor clothes, and Tony shone the beam into the opening while Gill struggled into the coat he had brought for her.

The strong beam showed them a rough passage carved out of the living rock. It descended steeply and was so lengthy that the torch could not penetrate the end.

Carefully they picked their way along the damp, evil-smelling passage. Tony led the way and, as they went on downwards, the rushing sound grew louder and more distinct.

"Gill, I believe we're going towards the sea."

A few minutes later, Tony's guess proved correct, as the thick, foul atmosphere gave way to draughts of fresh air carrying the unmistakable smell of the sea. The passage widened and finally opened out into a cave. Through the tiny entrance they could see the star-spangled sky and hear the rattling, rushing music of the waves as they hurled themselves against the beach.

Following the sides of the cave, they made for the opening and looked out. Below them the cliff dropped sheer and straight down to the beach—their own beach.

For a moment the children crouched on their knees, pondering this odd circumstance.

"Well, we had better look around," Tony said at last, and turned the torch to flood the cave with light.

The beam fell upon something which gleamed a hideous, yellowish-white, and Gill gave a little scream. In the far corner was a large iron-bound chest, and lying across it was the skeleton of a human. Here and there a few tattered remnants of blue and white cloth still clung to the bones, and an old pistol dangled from one bony finger.

With a shudder, Tony jerked the beam away from the gruesome sight, only to see the thin pencil of light fall upon yet another pile of human bones—with a gaping skull which seemed to be staring at them from wide, empty sockets.

Gill's courage seemed to have deserted her, for she shrank back against the damp wall and covered her face with her hands. Tony swung the torch, again sending the beam into the furthest corner of the cave.

"Here, Gill, look at this," he called suddenly.

"I can't, it's horrible," she answered.

"No, look over there, those little barrels—I think they're brandy kegs. I believe this was a smuggler's cave."

"Of course! The 'hazardous wealth from over the sea'. That's it, Tony! Old Sir Harry Mortlake made his fortune smuggling. This place was perfect for it. The boats could pull on to the beach without being seen, then the goods were hauled up here until Sir Harry could carry them through the secret passage to his house."

"Well, it looks as if his smuggling brought him to a

47

sticky end. He must have come down here one night, quarrelled with that other man, and in the fight they killed each other. No wonder Sir Harry vanished so mysteriously."

"Poor man," Gill said with soft pity. "For two hundred years he has haunted this place, waiting to show someone how to restore to the Mortlakes the only treasure he had to bequeath to his descendants."

"I think you're right. Come on, we mustn't touch anything—let's go and tell Mum and Dad everything."

The wavering torchlight bobbed and faded as the children hurried back up the passage, and behind them the cave receded once more into the darkness which had shrouded it for two centuries.

For some days following the children's discovery, Pontepelly House was a veritable hive of activity. Police, officials and other experts came and went, but at last the examinations were complete and a sad little procession headed by Sir Peter left the house bearing the remains of Sir Harry Mortlake to his last and final resting-place in the nearby churchyard.

Expert opinion had confirmed the children's guess. The cave was indeed a storehouse for smuggled goods, most of it mouldering and decayed. The chest which Sir Harry had apparently given his life to protect was found to be full of old coins, which by present-day values represented a small fortune, quite sufficient to keep Pontepelly House in the Mortlake family for ever.

"Well, it's all over now," Gill said. "We can enjoy the rest of our holiday in peace."

"No more funny voices in the night, eh, Gill?"

"No. But there is still one thing that puzzles me—why *me*? I mean, why did Sir Harry's ghost pick on me?"

"I think I can answer that." Tony and Gill turned as Sir Peter came into the room.

"I have been studying the old papers in the attic, and I have come across something rather interesting. I told you that the last time the clock started up was in my great-grandfather's time; well, apparently there was a little girl staying here then, and this child was taken home hurriedly because she began wandering in her sleep."

"Perhaps she was told to start up the clock, just like me."

"Yes, I believe so. And the odd thing was that her name was Jill."

"It rather looks as if Sir Harry had a weakness for that name."

Sir Peter laughed. "Yes, and I suppose that now we shall never know why."

"Well, I'm not going to ask him," Gill said. "I'm not going through all that again."

The rest of their happy holiday passed in an endless succession of glorious, sunlit days. Only one other odd circumstance occurred to puzzle them.

The great Mortlake clock began once more to measure out the passing hours, but this time it did not stop again, and as the Rowans finally closed the door of Pontepelly House at the end of their holiday, its long, slow, regular beat was the last sound they heard.

THE HAUNTED PILLAR-BOX

by ROSEMARY TIMPERLEY

THE snow was falling thinly as yet. Jim watched it from the classroom window. It looked so cool and he felt so hot. He'd been feeling seedy all day. Perhaps he'd caught a bug of some sort . . . "Jim, pay attention." The teacher's voice. "Sorry, Miss," he muttered. Then, to his relief, the bell rang for end of school.

"Hurry along," the teacher said. "Get home before we have a real snowstorm. I think one's coming." For the sky had turned leaden dark and already the snowflakes had grown as big as dandelion clocks.

Jim went to the cloakroom with the others, put on his cap and overcoat and set out into the whirling white world. He soon broke away from the main road into the network of suburban sidestreets where he lived. As the snow fell more thickly, he began to run, wanting to get home.

Running thus half-blind, he almost collided with her. Indeed he thought collision was inevitable, but she must have moved smartly aside, for he didn't even touch her. She was a pretty, pale-faced, black-haired woman, wearing a dark dress most inadequate for a winter's day, but she was carrying a big white fur muff, apparently to keep her fingers warm even if she didn't bother about the rest of her.

"Sorry, Miss," said Jim—today seemed to be all apologies. "I didn't see you. You appeared so suddenly."

She smiled, and a waft of lily-of-the-valley perfume came towards him. "Please," she said, "where is the pillar-box? I know it is near here. At the end of this street, perhaps?" She had a foreign accent.

"That's right," said Jim. "I'm going that way, so if you wanted to post a letter, I'll do it for you, then you can go back indoors." He presumed she'd dashed out of one of the houses in the street, grabbed her muff, but had not bothered to put a coat on. He admired her for the way she didn't seem to mind the snow. Most females are so fussy about weather. His mother tended to treat a shower of rain as if it were a raging tempest.

"I do not wish to post anything, *mon cher*," she said. "I wish to get inside the box." *Mon cher*. So she was French. He'd learned that much French at school.

"Get inside? To shelter, you mean? Oh, is it a phone-box you want, not a pillar-box?" He thought the poor foreigner might easily get the terms muddled.

"No, no," she said. "I wish not to climb into the box but to—to fetch something out of it."

"You can't do that in this country," said Jim. "Once something's in, it's in, unless you wait for the postman who collects, and even then there's a law against him passing anything over to you, because you might be someone else, mightn't you?"

He knew what he meant, but she looked puzzled.

"I don't mean you might be someone else, I mean you might not be the person you said you were, and what you were trying to get back might not be—" He lost track of the sentence. Words were the very devil. You knew what you meant, but finding the right words was like looking for a black thread in a dark room.

"Never mind, *chéri*," she said. "Take me to the pillar-box, please, and I will retrieve what was posted in great error."

He knew she wouldn't be able to do anything of the

sort, but he took her to the box. They stood and gazed at it. Already it had a high white hat of snow which made it seem taller than usual and almost human. Its gaping mouth looked as if it might say: "Hello. Cold, innit? Like my hat?"

"It's got a fluffy white hat like your muff," commented Jim.

"Soon I shall not need my muff," she said. "I will leave it for you when I have got my property back. Then I shall be complete and free to fly home."

"I wouldn't fancy flying in this weather," said Jim.

"Weather is nothing. An illusion."

"It doesn't seem very cold to me either," admitted Jim, "although I can see it must be. I'm as hot as pepper. You know, *Mademoiselle*—"

"*Madame*," she corrected him.

"*Madame*, we'll never get your property out, whatever it is, because it'll be at the bottom of the box, and we haven't got a fishing-rod or anything to put through the mouth."

He peered into the mouth of the box to see if, by any chance, the mail was stacked high. Last Christmas, for instance, that box had been so full that it had started to spit letters out! He saw nothing but the dark, however—and then something touched the bridge of his nose. It was a cold little caress, not alarming in itself, but startling in the circumstances. Jim sprang back with a cry.

"Something touched me! There must be an insect—or an animal on its hind legs—or a bird—"

"Two little white birds. That is what an artist once called my hands . . . my beautiful hands. Then my husband —the villain— he spoiled my beauty and posted it here. Well, as I said, now that I have found it, I am free to go home. Thank you for your kindness and your help. You are a gallant English gentleman—not like *him*, who was wicked and cruel." And she gave him the lightest of kisses on his forehead.

He noticed again the scent of lily-of-the-valley all about her. The fragrance seemed to mingle with the snowflakes so that he felt sprayed with iced perfume, deliciously comforting on his hot face.

Then she behaved very strangely. She thrust her left arm forward, placed her muff against the mouth of the box, and looked up at the sky, letting the snow fall full on her upturned features, blurring them, half-dissolving them in the snowflakes' whiteness. Jim looked up, too, following the direction of her gaze, but saw only the blinding snow. When he lowered his eyes again, she had gone.

He stood still as a snowman in his astonishment. How had she managed to run off so quickly? What had she retrieved from the pillar-box? *What* had touched him?

Now he noticed something that made his heart race with—not fear, exactly, but an awareness of the uncanny. He saw his own set of footprints, made when he'd approached the pillar-box, but not hers. Yet they had walked along together. Also, she had run off alone, yet there was no sign of her departing footprints.

What was happening to him? Was he dreaming or going mad or snow-bewitched?

Snow suddenly slithered from the top of the box to the ground. He jumped nervously at the swish of it and looked down at his feet. There he saw something which proved surely that he had not been dreaming. Of course she had been real! She had left her muff behind. He remembered her saying: "I will leave it for you when I have got my property back." She had kept her promise.

He picked up the muff in both hands, the white fur muff, cold with snow and fragrant with lily-of-the-valley. He stroked it and pressed it with his fingers, then placed his hot cheeks against it. He was feeling rather ill again, now that the excitement was over, for the fascinating French

53

woman had for a while taken his mind off his bodily discomfort.

A Post Office van loomed up, emerging from the snowfall like a monster. The postman climbed out and came to empty the box.

"Hello," he said to Jim. "What are you doing? Sunbathing?"

"Did you see a pretty French lady running along in a dark dress as you drove here?" Jim asked.

"I don't drink and drive," said the postman, unlocking the box and beginning to empty the letters and packets into his sack.

"I wasn't joking," said Jim. "She was here a minute ago, then she vanished. You might have seen her. Any feathers in there? Something gave me a sort of feathery touch on the nose when I looked in."

The postman was regarding him with concern. "Are you lost?"

"No, I'm not lost, only puzzled, and I do feel a bit swimmy. I've felt peculiar all day. I suppose you couldn't give me a lift home?" He recited his address.

"It's against the regulations, but . . . Oh, hop in. They can only shoot me at dawn once."

Gratefully, Jim clambered into the van and they began to drive through the snow. "Funny you should mention a French lady," the man said thoughtfully.

"Why?"

"It reminded me of something queer that happened years ago. I was new in the Post Office service. In fact, that was one of the first boxes I ever emptied. My mates had warned me about odd finds in pillar-boxes—apple-cores, old comics, bacon rinds, sausages, sets of false teeth—"

Jim burst out laughing.

"Oh, yes," grinned the man. "You name it, we find it,

sooner or later. But my first 'odd find', in that box, turned me over."

"What was it?" Jim asked eagerly. "A body? Ironed flat first," he added, remembering the size of a pillar-box's mouth.

"Not quite," said the man, "but a bit of one. I found a lady's left-hand little finger."

Wheeew, swished the snow on the roof of the van, and Jim echoed its sound. "Straight up?" he said.

"Straight up," said the postman.

"What did you do?"

"Wrapped it in a hanky and took it back to H.Q. They sent me along to the police station with it."

Jim was filled with envy. He had no idea a postman's life was so dramatic.

"And did you find out whose it was and how it got there?" he asked.

"I did. A very worried husband had turned up at the police station, saying his wife had left him because he took her finger. This is an outline of what had happened: He was a carpenter and she was a lady, like in the song. Only she was a French lady. Very pretty. Very vain. And especially vain about her hands, because some nut had once called them 'two little white birds'."

Jim gasped, then stayed silent, listening intently.

"One day she was fussing around him when he was try-ing to work, the way wives do. His hand slipped on the saw he was using, and it sliced off the little finger of her left hand."

Jim winced in sympathy for the victim of the accident.

"Well, of course, it was a terrible thing to happen," the man continued, "but an accident's an accident. There are worse things in life than losing a finger. A pal of mine lost one in the war and he doesn't think twice about it, and no one notices unless they look specially. But this lady cared desperately about her pretty hands, so she couldn't forgive her husband. They began to quarrel about everything, but especially over the fact that she kept the finger, in a special little box. He said that wasn't healthy and she should get rid of it. She refused. One night—the night before I found the finger—they had a real humdinger of a row, and he went berserk, took the finger, ran out of the house, didn't know what to do with it once he was out—so he posted it. Daft sort of thing to do, but he wasn't himself."

"What about her? She must have been very upset."

"Of course she was. He'd no right, you see. It was *her* finger. And when he got home, he wouldn't tell her what he'd done with it. Next day, she ran away from him, taking with her only the muff which she used to hide her hand. So he'd come to the police, hoping they'd help him find her."

"Did they?"

"No. If the police had to look for every runaway wife, they'd have no time for anything else. Oh, but the husband was distressed. I walked along with him afterwards. He said he wished he'd told her what he'd done with the finger, because sure as eggs is eggs he'd have found her at the Post Office, looking for it. And he said something . . ." The man hesitated.

"Go *on*," Jim urged him.

"He said: 'If I never find her, she won't know what happened to her missing finger until she dies, because after they die, people know the things they wanted to know when they were alive'. I think that's a bit of a sweeping statement myself."

Jim stayed quiet, then asked tensely, "And is she—dead?"

"Yes. After all these years without her, the husband was notified only the other day that she'd died of some virus infection, and the first thing he said was: 'Now she'll know that I posted her little finger.' Poor devil, he'd

56

been as haunted by it as she was. There's nowt so queer as folks, is there, son?"

Jim said nothing. He was thinking deeply, remembering things the French woman had said—such strange things—remembering how she had left no footprints, remembering how she had placed her muff against the mouth of the pillar-box and he had never seen her left hand at all—and then she had not needed her protective muff any longer, the guardian of her wounded vanity. It all made sense to him now.

"I've seen the ghost of that French lady," he announced. "Her husband was right. She did know that he'd posted her missing finger, and which pillar-box to look in. I helped her find it. Yes. It's wonderful! She came to collect her finger, then she was complete and free to go 'home' as she called it. Heaven, with luck. She mentioned flying, and she said the weather was an illusion." He spoke with quiet certainty, but he waited to be scoffed at, because adults usually scoff at anything out of the ordinary.

The postman, however, accepted his statement. "More things in heaven and earth, as they say," he said.

"You believe me?"

"Why not? We postmen see so many weird things ourselves that we believe everything. Now, here's your address, lad. Out you get."

Jim got out of the van. "Thanks a million for the lift. I hope you don't get shot at dawn!"

"I'll watch it," laughed the other.

The van swished off into the snowstorm.

In a daze, clutching the snow-covered muff, Jim entered the house. He left the muff on the hallstand and went into the kitchen.

"Change out of your wet things before tea, Jim," his mother said, barely turning her head from the stove. "Don't go bringing a lot of snow in here."

57

But Jim burst out, "Mum, I've had an adventure! I met a real live ghost!" He continued rapidly, trustingly: "She was the ghost of a French lady whose husband cut off her little finger accidentally and then posted it in *our* pillar-box and she came to collect it and I helped her— and it stroked my nose!"

His mother turned in alarm. "Sit down and be quiet." She fetched the thermometer and took his temperature. "A hundred and one. Straight up to bed with you. You're delirious, my love."

"But I *did* see this ghost. Perhaps when you're delirious you see things that you wouldn't normally see, but which are there all the time, and I saw—"

"Up to bed! Now!"

His father came in from work. "God, what weather!"

"Dad, I've seen a ghost—"

"He's got a raging temperature, poor chap," his mother explained.

"She left no footprints in the snow, and the postman said—"

They weren't listening. He told the story over and over, to his mother, his father, and later the doctor, who was sent for.

"There's a lot of it around," said the doctor. "Take these two little pills and go right off to sleep—and no more silly ghost dreams, eh?"

It was a conspiracy of adults. With their disbelief they almost convinced *him* that he'd had a dream-awake—that none of it had really happened. Then, just as he was drifting off to sleep, he remembered the muff. They'd find that when he was asleep, realise that it was proof of the lady's existence, and believe him . . .

When he awoke, it was morning. The world was still and white outside. A primrose sun struggled through the blanched air. His mother brought his breakfast.

"How are you, darling?"

"Better. Did you find the white fur muff I left on the hall-stand? It's hers."

"You're a naughty boy. You left a huge snowball on the hallstand and it melted all over the place. Still, you weren't well. You didn't know what you were doing."

"It *was* a muff! I expect ghost-things change overnight. It was *her* muff! It was! And I did see her!"

"Oh, you're incorrigible!" She was half-laughing, half-angry. "There are no such things as ghosts, and if there are, they certainly don't appear to little boys."

"But I—"

"No! That's enough. It was a hallucination, a vision seen in fever, and nothing more. One day you'll read some psychiatry, Jim, and understand about hallucinations. Drunks have them too, and climbers on high mountains, and people who've been without sleep for a long time. It's a not uncommon medical phenomenon. One thing is for certain, there was no ghostly French lady, and the so-called white fur muff was only a snowball."

Jim sank back wearily against the pillow. "Okay," he said wearily. "You win, talking all that jargon." Then he had a last, silent, very intense wish in his head: Please, please, beautiful *Madame*, walk in here now and prove her wrong. Do it for *me*. Please!

He closed his eyes and waited. Nothing happened for a second, then, suddenly, there was a faint movement of air—and the room was filled with the scent of lily-of-the-valley. Jim opened his eyes. His lady was not visible—but her scent! He said nothing.

He saw his mother pause in the doorway and sniff the air.

"I can smell lilies-of-the-valley," she said, "or lily-of-the-valley perfume. Have you brought some scent in here?"

"No," said Jim.

"Then where's it coming from?"

59

He opened his lips to say, "It's my French lady who found her lost finger in our haunted pillar-box—" Then he changed his mind. He decided to get his own back in a more subtle way.

"I can't smell anything, Mum," he said innocently. "You must be having one of those hallucinations. Maybe it runs in the family."

She gave him a look and left the room.

"Merci, Madame," he whispered to the invisible presence, and felt on the bridge of his nose a cool, half-teasing caress, as if from the ghost of a lady's little finger.

DREAM GHOST

by SYDNEY J. BOUNDS

MANDY awoke suddenly in the night, trembling with fear. Moonlight flooded her bedroom with silver and shadow. It was only a dream, she told herself, only a dream. So why was she shivering in a warm bed?

A memory of the dream returned and she threw back the bedclothes and switched on the light. It had all seemed so real, and she'd never had a fright like that before.

She wrapped a dressing-gown around her and opened the door. The house was quiet, the passage in darkness, as she felt her way along the wall to her brother's room. She opened the door and closed it behind her, switched on the light.

Joe's room was full of aeroplane models, and she had to move carefully to avoid them. She sat on the edge of his bed and shook him hard; Joe was a heavy sleeper.

Presently, her brother stirred. "What's up, then? Mandy . . ."

"I had a nightmare, Joe. It scared me—I've got to talk to somebody."

Joe was twelve, two years younger than his sister, and sturdy, with unruly fair hair.

Mandy shuddered. "It was horrid!"

Joe sat up reluctantly; he was still sleepy. "What was it about?"

"I was walking alone, through a mist, and all round me were ruins. It was nowhere I've ever seen, I'm sure of that. And then *she* came towards me, through the mist.

Her feet didn't touch the ground—she just drifted along. I could see right through her, Joe. She was a ghost, a girl of about my age in a long dress, and with a pale face. Her mouth was moving as if she was trying to say something, but I couldn't hear what it was—like watching the old silent movies on telly. That's all, really, because I woke up. But it was so real." She forced a laugh. "I don't know why I was scared so much—it was only a dream."

Joe rubbed sleep from his eyes and looked hard at his sister. "You do look a bit white . . . Still, I never heard of anyone dreaming a ghost before." He sounded impressed.

Mandy stood up. "I'll be all right now, Joe. Thanks for listening."

She tiptoed back to her room, and it was a long time before she fell asleep.

A week later, Mandy dreamed again. She stood among the ruins of an old house and it was dark. The ghost girl appeared before her, rippling as if seen through water. She felt icy cold. The ghost drifted nearer and lifted an arm, reaching out a hand to touch her . . .

Mandy awoke abruptly, soaked with sweat, her heart thumping wildly. She pushed bedclothes into her mouth to stop herself screaming. It was ridiculous, she thought, scared silly by a dream . . .

At the breakfast table, her mother commented: "You look off-colour, Mandy. Are you sleeping all right?"

Joe hastily swallowed a spoonful of cereal. "Was it the dream again?"

Their father looked up from his newspaper crossword. "What dream's this? First I've heard of it."

"She dreamed a ghost," Joe said proudly.

"A ghost?" Father looked interested. "That's jolly original."

Mother said, "Well, don't do it again if it's going to make you ill."

Mandy made a silent prayer that she would never dream that particular dream again. Ever.

Another week passed before the dream returned. This time Mandy was exploring overgrown shrubbery in the large garden surrounding the ruins. And when the ghost girl reached out a hand to touch her, the ground opened and Mandy fell into darkness. She was falling, falling . . .

She woke up screaming. The bedroom door opened and the light came on. Mother came in hurriedly, looking concerned.

"What is it, Mandy?"

"The dream," she sobbed. "The ghost came for me again!"

Mother put her arms around her, and gradually she quietened down. "I'll leave the light on—and in the morning I'm taking you to see Dr. Thomson. We can't have this going on any longer."

Dr. Thomson was a chubby little man with a red face and bushy grey hair. After he'd listened to Mandy's story, he admitted: "This is a new one on me. Let's see now, you break up for the holidays soon—are you going away?"

"To Devon, to stay with an uncle. That's next week."

"Not next week," the doctor said briskly. "Right now. Today. There's nothing like a change of air and a bit of exercise. Perhaps you've been studying too hard."

At home, Father made a phone call while Mother packed two cases. Mandy and Joe got in the car, waving goodbye to Mother as they drove off.

Mandy began to feel better already as the car gathered speed on the main road to Exeter.

"It'll be fun," Joe said. "Uncle George and Ben and Polly. And Dartmoor to explore."

Uncle George was an artist and designed sleeves for pop records; he was easy-going and the children could do what they liked. He was a widower and had only recently moved to a cottage on Dartmoor.

It was late afternoon when they arrived, driving across the desolate moor to a small cottage set beside a stream between hills. Pop music blared from a record-player. The children, Ben and Polly, came running out to greet them.

"Now we can have fun!" Ben shouted.

Mandy's father stayed for a meal before driving home, and Uncle George told him: "She'll be all right here. A few days on the moor and she'll be too exhausted to dream. My two sleep like logs."

It began to seem that Uncle George was right. In the days that followed, the four children explored the wild moor, hunting for bronze-age relics and barrows, chasing wild ponies, climbing the high tors. There was Devon cream for tea, and Mandy's skin turned nut-brown in the sun and wind; she felt fitter than she'd ever felt before—and the dream didn't come back to bother her.

Uncle George was at his easel, immersed in a new painting, and Polly and Mandy were cutting sandwiches. Ben announced: "Today we're going to the old house for a picnic. It's a super place to play hide-and-seek."

"O.K. kids," Uncle George said absently. "Mind you get back before dark."

It was a bright sunny day when they set out, walking between ferns and yellow-flowering gorse. Ben, who had short legs and was inclined to be on the tubby side, complained: "Not so fast."

"Oh, come on Fatty!"

"Shut your face, Pretty Poll!"

Polly—who *was* pretty—ran ahead, blonde hair streaming. "Can't catch me!"

The moor was empty of life except for some sheep in the distance.

"What's this old house?" Joe asked.

"It's not a house really, not any more. Just the ruins of

64

The ghost girl reached out a hand to touch her . . .

one. But there are lots of walls standing, and thick shrubbery. No one ever goes there, so we'll have the place to ourselves."

When they reached the ruins, all four were hungry, and Mandy and Polly set out their picnic lunch.

Mandy was finishing her sandwiches and drinking lemonade when she began to look around with fresh interest. She had the eerie feeling she knew this place; but that was impossible—she'd never been on Dartmoor before. The feeling persisted and the memory of her dream returned.

All at once she began to shiver. This was the place she'd dreamed . . .

Joe asked: "Are you all right, Mandy?"

She nodded. "It's just that this place reminds me of my dream. I'll get over it." She jumped to her feet. "Come on, let's play hide-and-seek."

"I'll be seeker first," Joe said.

Mandy and Ben and Polly ran off to hide while Joe shut his eyes and began to count to a hundred.

Mandy ran towards the shrubbery; it was thick and green with a lot of cover to hide in. Yet, as she approached, she felt curiously reluctant to enter the dark bushes. Behind her, Joe finished counting and called:

"Look out—I'm coming!"

Mandy took a deep breath and forced her way into the matted undergrowth. She moved slowly and quietly, and the green leaves closed above her head, shutting out the sun. She began to feel cold and lonely. She pressed deeper and deeper into the shrubbery, following what might once have been a path but was now grown over with weeds and wild flowers.

Far enough, Mandy thought—Joe won't find me here. She took a few more steps forward, and then . . .

Mist curled up from the ground in front of her and shaped itself into a human figure. Mandy stopped dead,

66

her heart in her mouth. She was looking at the ghost girl of her dreams, a young girl wearing an old-fashioned frock. Her face was pale and her expression sad. The ghost wavered in the air before Mandy's staring eyes—and she could see dark green leaves through the wraith.

The ghost shimmered as it drifted towards her. Mandy stood paralysed, her legs turned to jelly. A slender arm was lifted and a hand reached out, touched her. The touch was as cold as ice, and it burned.

Mandy jumped. She turned and bolted in panic crashing through the bushes till she burst out into sunshine and collapsed on the grass.

Joe raced up, calling: "Mandy! What's the matter?"

"The ghost, Joe . . . I saw her." She pointed to the bushes. "In there."

"I'm going to look," Joe said fiercely. "I'll settle that old ghost." He went into the shrubbery, determined, but moving warily.

Ben and Polly joined Mandy as Joe returned. He had a thoughtful expression on his face. "I didn't see your ghost," he said. "What I did see was a dark, deep well. So it was lucky you did see her just then. We've got to tell Uncle George about this."

Next day, Uncle George and a policeman visited the hidden well. At the bottom they found the skeleton of a young girl, which was later brought up and buried in the local churchyard.

How terrible, Mandy thought, to die like that.

She never dreamed of her ghost-girl again, though she tried. She would have liked the ghost to come back—just once—so she could thank the girl for saving her life. In a strange way, she knew she had lost a friend.

But Mandy never forgot her. She was reminded of her every time she looked at her wrist, at the marks that never completely faded—marks left where ghostly fingers had touched her.

CRUSOE'S PARROT

by RICK FERREIRA

"ROBIN! Robin!" my mum said.

She called my name softly, as if the last thing she wanted to do was to wake me. "Rob . . . will you come for a swim?" And when I still pretended to be asleep, she shook me gently and kind of whispered: "It *is* our last day on the island, so will you try to be happy—for my sake?"

I opened my eyes then and her face, very brown and shiny, was just above mine, and her eyes had that worried look again. The look that had started at Dad's funeral— and now it was always there, whenever she looked at me. Worried and tensed up. Yet what did she think I'd do? Burst into tears? Make a scene? The car crash had killed Dad. I knew *now* just how final that was. And, anyway, I was twelve and kids my age don't cry that easy. At least, they make sure they don't get caught at it . . .

But the great big lump in my throat was always there —whenever I thought of him for more than a few seconds —and it was hard to swallow then. You see, Tobago, this island we're on, had been my dad's island. He was born on this island, and ever since I can remember he had wanted to bring Mum and me back here on a holiday visit. "It's Crusoe's island, too. Robinson Crusoe lived on Tobago for twenty-seven years!" Then my dad would go on, grinning at me—"And it was so beautiful he never had the time to be lonely. Of course, he had his parrot, and, much later, Man Friday came along. It's a great island

68

if you want to be a castaway. Robin, boy, you've got a great experience coming up one day . . ."

Well, I was having the great holiday at last, without Dad, and feeling lonely all the time. *I* hadn't a parrot or a Man Friday. All I had were the other tourists who had come for a fortnight on Tobago, on a Boeing 707, all the way from London. And I missed Dad, for I wanted to discuss things like cruising speed, air turbulence, and what would really happen if one of the engines fell out. I swallowed hard, up there, high in the clouds, and then the loneliness started and I couldn't get rid of it. And it just got worse really, with each day so bright and hot— yet kind of empty.

And then I began to notice that Mum was already beginning to forget Dad, for she was laughing a lot with Mr. John Hartman.

So I looked up at her and said, "Why don't you ask Mr. John Hartman instead? He's never gone into the sea —but he might for *you*!" And then I watched her go very still and her smile fade away, then she blinked a few times and bit her lip.

I was sorry, then. I wanted to grab her hand, or hug her, or—or something. At least, I never meant to say what I found myself saying: "I hate Mr. John Hartman! He's fat and—and he's got too much hair!" But by then Mum had turned away and gone back through the door into her bedroom.

It was the room she was to share with Dad while I had this small bedroom. I wasn't a little kid after all. And we had picked this kind of beach-bungalow from the holiday brochure about Tobago. You walked out from the bungalow straight on to the sand, then past the umbrella-shelters made of coconut branches, then right into the blue sea. And the waiter would bring you a Coke, or the housemaid bring you ice-cream in a coconut-shell. Ice cream that tasted like *real* banana.

This hot greeny West Indian island was exactly as Dad had talked on and on about, ever since I really started listening. And one day he bought me my very own copy of *The Adventures of Robinson Crusoe*—then the book, and Tobago, and my dad, all became one in my mind. I wasn't clever then; I was seven or eight. And now it was all real . . . the heat and the sunlight, the birds and the flowers, the coconut-trees and the bungalows. But it was kind of unreal, too, because of Dad being missing.

I was having to swallow that great lump again, so I sprang out of bed, stripped off my pyjamas and raced into the shower, through the small passage behind our bedrooms. Then I turned on the cold tap and felt really good as the water lashed out at me, and then I looked right into the stream and caught it full on my face.

Then, on the curve of the shower, right above the spray —I saw a parrot!

A large parrot, all green and yellow and black, and its head was cocked to one side as it looked down at me. My mouth must have fallen open, because I swallowed a lot of water, then I shouted: "Mum! Mum! Come quickly, *please*. There's a great big parrot in the shower!"

And someone did come into the shower, but it was Milly, the West Indian maid who cleaned up our bungalow every day. And Milly and I were great friends—we were friends from the moment we had met on the first day of the holiday. Milly had started calling me "Sonny Boy" in minutes.

"What parrot is this?" Milly asked, keeping clear of the spray. "We don't allow animals or birds in the bungalows. You'd better hurry . . . your mother ordered the breakfast for nine o'clock. You should have gone swimming *then* have a shower."

I skipped out of the shower, and Milly gave me a fresh towel, but I hardly noticed. "A great big parrot! It's *up there*!" I shouted. "Can't you see it, Milly? It's beautiful, isn't it?"

Then I looked at Milly and she was looking at me. Kind of on her guard. "There's no parrot in this shower!" Milly said in a no-nonsense voice. "Now dry yourself, Sonny Boy, and get dressed. I can hear your mother next door. She didn't go for a swim either, so she'll want breakfast." And Milly took up the two towels from yesterday and rolled out of the shower. But the parrot *was* there, I looked at it all the time I was drying myself.

Then I ran back into my bedroom and started looking in the big suitcase for my red tee-shirt with *Tobago* on it—and when I looked up, there was the parrot on my bed. And I hadn't seen it fly out of the shower or anything. But now it was there, on the headboard.

And doing tricks!"

It swung right through the bamboo bars in the headboard, hanging by just one foot, while the shiny black head and yellow beak looked crookedly up at me. And then it said, croakily, but clear as my transistor, "Poor Robin! Poor Robin!" And then it winked one red eye—shiny like a button—and with its free foot began to scratch the tuft of black feathers on its head!

It was the funniest thing I'd ever seen, and I burst out laughing. I laughed so loudly that Mum came rushing into my room, with Milly waddling close behind her.

"Robin! Are you all right?" Then Mum looked around, quite bewildered, and Milly looked at me, too, but with a funny, wise kind of look.

It was then that I realized that neither of them could *see* the parrot! And the parrot chose that very moment to wink again at me and say: "Poor Robin Selkirk!"

And that started me laughing again, and then I knew that I had to tell them something or they'd think that I'd gone crackers. *Anything*— So I said, "It's just one of Dad's jokes. I don't know why I should remember it right now . . ." And Mum remembered the funny man my dad had been and she smiled back at me. She looked suddenly very happy and relieved and I felt glad. Her eyes weren't anxious either.

"Oh, Rob! I—I miss the jokes, too!" And she suddenly hugged me very tight and laughed, because I was still laughing. "And now, darling—*breakfast*. I'm very hungry and I know you must be too. We'll have Milly bring it around in a few minutes and eat on the verandah. O.K.?"

"O.K.!" I said, then Mum let me go and went away, smiling.

But Milly stayed. And Milly said, very quiet and soft: "I know that you're seeing Crusoe's parrot. It's real to you. It only comes to the lonely and unhappy people, but they don't stay that way very long. You ain't afraid, are you?"

I shook my head. I hadn't thought of being afraid.

"Is it a *ghost* parrot, Milly? The ghost of the parrot that Robinson Crusoe had here—on Tobago? Years and years ago?"

"Yes," Milly said, still in the hushed voice. "It'll stay with you just this one day. Then, come sundown, it will go. Or he'll come to collect the parrot—"

"Poor Robin Selkirk!" the parrot said, walking like a drunken sailor over my pillow. Then it stopped and lowered its head on to the pillow, then winked at me yet again. And the sweeping green and blue feathers of its tail spread open like a fan.

That parrot was the best comic I'd ever seen!

I laughed so much I had to grab hold of Milly. And like Mum, she was smiling, too, her teeth shiny white in her round, black face. "Hush, Sonny Boy!" Milly said. "Your mother is bound to suspect something if you go on laughing like that all the day. Now, you just let go of me and I'll get the breakfast."

But I held on to her. "Tell me just one thing more. Milly, if he comes for the parrot—will I actually see Robinson Crusoe? Will I?"

"Yes," Milly said, rolling her eyes. "When you can see the one then you'll see the other. And you'll be a happy boy once again before you leave this island. You mark my words!"

After that we had breakfast.

And while Mum and I ate, the parrot hung upside down from a roof beam on the verandah and made rude noises. And winked when I tried not to laugh. Then we went out to the beach and I left Mum at her favourite spot, under the big umbrella shelter of dried palm leaves, and I ran straight into the warm blue water. And the parrot flew out to sea, right over my head.

Then we started a great game of battleship and dive-bomber. The parrot would dive, out of the sun, making straight for me, and I would swim madly and turn and twist—making myself a hard target to hit. It was the best time I'd had in the sea since that holiday in Cornwall, with Dad, when I was nine. I didn't want to come out of the sea, but Mum finally sent Mr. John Hartman to call me in for an ice-cream in a coconut shell.

"You're quite the young swimmer, Robin!" Mr. John Hartman said, but I noticed that he didn't go much deeper into the sea than up to his knees. He put his hand on my wet shoulder as we walked together up to Mum's umbrella-shelter, and all the time he was smoothing his hair down with the other hand. He was very proud of all that hair. My Dad had been almost bald—ever since I could remember—and that had seemed right, somehow. Well, fathers should be almost bald. Not with a great mass of curly hair like Mr. John Hartman . . .

As we came nearer to Mum I saw that the parrot had got ahead of me, as usual. It was sliding down the roof of coconut leaves, then stopping itself by biting firmly

73

with its beak, just before it fell to the sand. I watched it do the trick twice and it looked twice as funny, so I laughed. I just couldn't help it.

Mr. John Hartman squeezed my shoulder.

"I'm so glad you're happier today, Robin. Your mother has been quite concerned about you. It's our last day on Tobago, so enjoy it while—" Then suddenly Mr. John Hartman said something like, "Ohhhhhh . . ."

And it had happened all in a flash.

A flash of yellow and green and black . . . as the parrot flew straight at us and its claws sank into Mr. John Hartman's curly hair. And then it flew straight out to sea, taking the great pile of hair with it!

Mr. John Hartman just stood there in the sun with a head as shiny as a conker, and his face was a bright, bright red. Then he mumbled something at Mum and turned and started racing up the sand, looking madly to right and left as he ran and ran.

Mum looked quite stunned by it all, but only for a moment.

"Oh, Rob! The poor man is *bald*. Your father had twice as much hair!" And Mum rocked in the bamboo seat with the bright red cushions. I was laughing, too, for I could see something that no one else could. The parrot had done a U-turn and was now heading back for the beach, then it dropped the wig on a group of girls who were sun-bathing not very far from our shelter. "People shouldn't wear those things on a windy beach," Mum said, laughing again. It was really a happy kind of laugh. The way she'd laugh at Dad's jokes, with her head right back and her eyes shiny. I knew then that really she hadn't liked Mr. John Hartman that much . . .

And suddenly I felt great. Really great. For I had Mum to myself and this sunny last day I wasn't lonely or sad. And—would you believe it?—the parrot chose that very moment to fly back and settle on the sand under our shelter. But, being the true comic, it had to go in to some kind of act. So it started scratching a deep hole in the sand, then it buried its head in the hole. But I still heard it croaking, quite plainly: "Poor Robin! Poor Robin!"

And Mum laughed with me again as she handed over my ice-cream in the coconut shell. "Rob—do try to stay this way," she said. "Your dad was always a happy man. Let's try not to let him down any more . . ."

"It's all over, Mum," I said, knowing that it was true, and feeling very glad that it was. And Mum nodded then bit her lip and I knew that she was about to go all weepy, so I reached down and gave her the beach-bag. But that was O.K., really. Mums should be weepy sometimes, just as dads should be almost bald. All of the time.

And I still felt great when that last day on Dad's island came to an end and the sun went down into the sea and it seemed to go dark in seconds. Everyone was in their bungalows getting ready for the farewell "limbo" party, but I stood at my bedroom window and watched the sand and the sea and the umbrella shelters all slowly disappear.

And I watched the parrot, too, as it sat, very still, on the rail that ran along the verandah. Then it suddenly flapped its wings and took off, straight as an arrow, heading for the empty beach. But then I saw that the beach wasn't *completely* empty, for I could see a tall figure, dressed all in goatskins from head to toe, standing far out at the water's edge.

I could see him dimly and yet very clearly, too, and the parrot flew straight to him. It circled once over the funny, tall figure, then it flapped down on to a goatskin-covered shoulder. Then slowly they began to move on, at the very edge of the sea, and I couldn't see clearly any more. Then the dark swallowed them up.

I stayed at the window until a firefly, all glowing and winking, shot past me into the bedroom. So I closed the mesh window, then the real one. It was all over, really.

75

"Robin, boy, you've got a great experience coming up . . ." My dad had said that so many times. "Just wait until you get to my island!"

Well, Tobago had given me a great experience, and it was hard keeping it all to myself, so, on the plane, I did try to tell Mum. It was just after I'd asked the stewardess if she had ever been on a hijacked flight and did the hijacker have a gun *and* a bomb? Then Mum said in her apologising voice: "My son has quite an imagination! Robin, do stop asking silly questions."

The stewardess winked at me, but by then I'd got rather worried. Well, had I actually imagined that parrot . . . and its owner, all in goatskins, who had come to claim it? So I said, all in a rush. "Mum! Something very weird happened yesterday. *I saw Robinson Crusoe and his parrot!*"

Mum sighed and stopped looking out at the bright clouds. But she smiled when our eyes met. "You're being silly again. Robinson Crusoe is just a character in a book. His parrot is just make-believe, too. Someone just thought up all those adventures—"

"Daniel Defoe," I said. "That was the name of the man who wrote the book."

"Yes," Mum said. "Yes, now I remember. Anyway, it's all *fictitious*—so how could you possibly see Crusoe or his parrot?" Then she patted my hand as if I were still seven and really dim. Mums are like that sometimes. "I'm going to try to get some sleep now . . ." Well, I gave up completely then, but just before she closed her eyes, my Mum said, "Tobago was everything your dad said. I'm so glad we came, Rob . . ."

"So am I," I said, but her eyes were closed by then. And when I thought of my dad, I found that there was no big lump to swallow. Even when I remembered the heavy feel of his hand on my head. He was fond of doing that, even when I got so tall. Then, naturally, I thought

76

of that great clown of a parrot, Crusoe's parrot, and suddenly I started laughing, out loud.

"Hush, Rob!" Mum said, still with her eyes shut. "You'll have everyone looking. Is it another of your dad's jokes?"

"Yes," I said, and I patted *her* hand. "It's the one about a parrot. A very funny parrot."

THE GIRL IN THE MIRROR

by Margot Arnold

JENNIFER VIDLER looked around her room with a sigh of
boredom.

It was untidy, as usual, but she could not be bothered
to tidy it up, even though her mother had been after her
to do so. Her friends were always going on about how
pretty it was and how lucky she was to have a room like
this of her own. Little did *they* know, she thought gloomily.
Her eyes wandered over the bleached silver-oak fittings:
the built-in wardrobe, the desk, the bookshelves and the
stand that held her stereo and television set, and moved on
to the gracious lines of her white four-poster bed that
seemed almost to float on the thick scarlet wall-to-wall
carpet.

She went slowly to the window and gazed down at the
busy street below. From this height, cars and people
looked like large mechanical toys moving jerkily and without purpose. Oh, what she would give to be away from
all this, away from the city! Right away in the country.
She slipped easily into her favourite daydream—a big
farm in the country with her own horse, and a dog, and
cats, and rabbits, and lots of space to roam around in,
and—oh, everything! Roaming wild and free all day long
with the animals . . . A horn honked outside and the dream
shattered.

Again she sighed heavily. Here it was, the beginning
of the summer holidays, and all she had to look forward

to was a measly fortnight in France with her parents. She was almost sorry that school was finally over—not that she liked school that much, but at least it was something to *do*.

She put a David Cassidy record on the turntable and continued her restless ramble around the room. Coming to the dressing-table with its glass top and white-flounced frill, she stopped before it and, propping her head in her hands, gazed moodily into the mirror. She had made a fuss about it when her mother had put it in the room, but secretly she rather liked it. It had been one of the "heirlooms" she had inherited from her great-aunt and namesake, Aunt Jennifer, and it did not quite "go" with the rest of the room, being an antique, shield-shaped, swing-mirror, standing on its own little stand in which were three small velvet-lined drawers where she kept her most cherished possessions.

Every time she looked into it she would think of Aunt Jennifer, who had been incredibly old but who had always interested her with stories about her long-gone youth on a farm in Kent. What especially interested young Jennifer were the stories her great-aunt used to tell about her own grandmother, who had lived on the very same farm way back in the 1830s. She too, had been a Jennifer, and had had a twin sister called Belinda to whom something terrible had happened.

It had been a very long time before young Jennifer had managed to find out what that terrible thing was, because whenever her great-aunt got to that part, some grown-up— usually her own mother—would break in with, "Now I'm sure you don't want to go into all that, Aunt Jennifer," and their warning glances were enough to tell her that it was something they did not want her to know about. She had imagined all sorts of horrible things so, when at last she had got Aunt Jennifer all to herself and had heard the story, she had been quite disappointed.

"Oh," said Aunt Jennifer vaguely. "About poor Belinda? Yes, well she went quite mad when she was a young girl and had to spend the rest of her life shut up in the farm attic where no one could see her. They didn't know what to do with mad people in those days, you see, and it was a *terrible* disgrace to have one in the family."

"What made her go mad?" Jennifer asked with interest.

Her great-aunt shrugged. "My grandmother never knew for sure. She thought maybe it was because their stepmother was too hard on Belinda, who was a very dreamy kind of girl and who wasn't very helpful about the farm. Anyway, one summer's day Belinda started to act very strangely; she pretended she was Jennifer and talked about all kinds of crazy things like talking boxes and wheels that sang songs, and even about men flying about in the sky. It got so bad that they sent the real Jennifer, my grandmother, away for a while, and when she came back poor Belinda was chained up in the attic and she was never allowed to see her again, even though they were twins—and identical twins at that . . ."

Oh yes, Jennifer sorely missed Aunt Jennifer and her stories, but the old lady had died a few months ago and had left her some very nice things.

The door opened and her mother's face appeared around the crack. "Jennifer, *do* turn down that record-player! We'll have the neighbours complaining again." The head swivelled and took in the untidy state of the room. "And for goodness' sake, tidy this mess up, will you? It's the third time I've spoken to you about it." The voice was pained.

"All right," Jennifer said sullenly. Her mother sighed and closed the door with an exasperated click.

"Drat the neighbours!" Jennifer resumed her former position and stared dismally into the mirror. "Oh, how heavenly it must have been to live on that farm, away from everybody!" Her own sad face stared back at her.

the long dark hair hanging forward and slightly shadow-ing its pallor. Then she felt a thrill of amazement, for while the face was the same, the whole room behind was quite different. She glanced quickly over her shoulder to see if her eyes were playing tricks with her, but there was her own room, just the same as it always was. She looked back at the mirror, and the other room was still there—cream walls with great black beams showing in them, and dark, heavy furniture, including a large four-poster bed with a patchwork quilt. And there was a window where no window existed in her room; a window of small, diamond-shaped panes which stood open to show the leaves of a great oak tree dancing in the summer breeze, and there was a door of black oak with a latch instead of a knob on it.

Jennifer took each detail in slowly. How could this be? Here she was looking at her reflection in a strange room! Then she noticed with a shock that while the face was the same, the dress was quite different. The girl in the mirror was wearing a shapeless long dress of some kind of checked cotton, with stupid-looking puffed sleeves out of which her thin arms stuck like sticks. Jennifer glanced down at her own stylish nylon blouse and neat Black Watch kilt, then back at the mirror. "Who are you?" she whispered through dry lips. "Why is everything suddenly so different?"

The girl's face—her own face—came a little closer. "Oh, I'm *so* glad you've finally seen me; that you've said something!" The voice was high and thin and clear like a mountain stream. "Now we can talk. Now I can find out about all those wonderful things you have that I can see from here. I've been *dying* to know about them." She gave a delighted laugh that tinkled like a fairy bell. "What *talks* we'll be able to have now!"

"But . . . *where* are you?" Jennifer stammered.

"Why, on Pear Tree Farm, of course, where I've always

81

"Who are you?" she whispered.

been." The tinkly laugh broke out again. "And I know who *you* are; there's only one person in the world who looks exactly like me, so you're Jennifer. Don't you know me, silly? I'm Belinda!"

Thrills went up and down Jennifer's spine. "The farm —the old farm! You're actually on it?"

"Of course."

Jennifer looked very carefully at her look-alike, thinking of the sad story she had been told. She certainly did not *look* mad, and besides, behind her was the enchanting prospect of the farm. Belinda would be able to tell her all about it. "Well, I'm not *your* Jennifer," she said cautiously, "but I think I know what has happened. We are both of us caught in a Time Warp—that must be it!" (She was a great fan of *Star Trek*, so knew all about such things.)

"I don't care who you say you are, Jennifer, or what we're caught in, just so long as we can be friends and you can tell me all about those exciting things," Belinda said eagerly.

"I do know one thing, though," Jennifer went on. "We'll have to keep this a *deadly* secret between us. It would never do if anyone else found out."

"No, indeed!" Belinda made a face and shivered. "Why, my stepmother is so strict and nasty—well, she'd probably smash this glass if she thought I was having any *fun*."

So began their strange, looking-glass friendship. Jennifer's parents could hardly believe the change in her; instead of complaining all the time as she usually did in the holidays, she seemed perfectly content to stay in her room, and had almost to be pushed out of the flat to get some fresh air. "She really is becoming much more grown-up," her mother said proudly, and as a reward gave her a lovely gold locket with her birth-stone set in the middle of it.

As for Jennifer, she could hardly wait to get back to her room and the mirror, and to hear all the marvellous things about the farm. She would get quite cross with Belinda who, after a while, would always say: "I've talked enough. Now *you* tell *me* about your wonderful life." And she could not understand why Belinda should be so impressed by very ordinary things like having a bed all to oneself, and light whenever one needed it, or music at the touch of a switch. "Imagine! Music whenever you want it—what bliss! I do love it so, and there is none here on the farm, none at all," Belinda would say sadly.

But most of all it was her television set that really enchanted Belinda, who could not see enough of it and who made Jennifer very angry when she wanted to watch it instead of talking. She got so fed up with Belinda's constant pleas to see it that she would leave it on when she was not in the room, so that Belinda could watch. She was roundly scolded by her mother for wasting electricity, but she still went on doing it.

On her part, although she never tired of hearing about the two riding-horses and the dogs and cats, Jennifer became aware that farm life was not always as nice as she had imagined. Often when she hurried to the mirror Belinda would not be there, and when she did come she would be tired and cross. "I've been working," she would say irritably. "That's all there ever is to do here—work, work, work!" Her hands were always red and raw and quite ugly, but Jennifer was too polite to say so. And she found to her surprise that Belinda was quite ignorant about even the simplest things.

"Don't they teach you *anything* in school," she said crossly, one day when Belinda seemed even denser than usual.

"School?" echoed Belinda. "I don't go to school. That's just for *boys*. Though my grandmother did teach me how

84

to make the alphabet and sign my name on a sampler in needlework—*and* I know my figures," she said proudly. "I can add! You mean *you* go to school just like a boy, all the time?"

"Well, except for holidays," Jennifer agreed. "But it isn't any fun stuck in a stuffy old classroom every day. I *hate* it. You're lucky not to be bothered with it."

But the more they talked, the more they became envious of each other's life and unhappy with their own; especially Belinda, who would lapse into a gloomy silence and gaze longingly into Jennifer's room. One day when she was doing this, Jennifer cast around in her mind for something new to talk about. She opened up one of the velvet-lined drawers under the mirror and held up the new locket. "Look what my mother just gave me," she said.

Belinda brightened up. "Oh, it's just *beautiful*," she gasped, and reached for it. For a second a small misty hand appeared, and suddenly there was the locket on the other side of the mirror, with Belinda laughing and twirling it in the air.

"Hey!" said Jennifer. "You've taken my locket. Give it back!"

Belinda stopped laughing, and a look of wild hope came into her face. "Jenny," she whispered, "it *did* pass through. And if *it* can, maybe *we* can, too! Oh, wouldn't that be fun! I could get into your room and play with all those lovely things, and you could come here and play with the animals—even ride the horses, if you like."

"Well, I don't know," Jennifer said dubiously. "Do you think it would work?"

"Why not? Let's see if I can give the locket back . . ." Again a misty outline appeared, and there was the locket gleaming on the glass top. "See, Jenny! I believe we could. Let's try it. You put your fingers to mine on the glass, and when I say 'Go', we'll both take two steps forward."

85

The idea had begun to excite Jennifer. "All right," she said eagerly, then another thought struck her. "But wait a moment! What about our clothes? We'd look pretty weird to anyone else. I mean, what would my mother say if she came in and saw you in that cotton sack thing."

Belinda thought for a minute and chuckled. "Then we'll take our clothes off, and when we get to the other side we'll dress in one another's. Then, when we're ready to come back, we'll change again."

Jennifer's heart pounded with excitement. "Right," she whispered, and started to undress a bit shamefacedly, her fingers trembling nervously. At last they faced one another, giggling self-consciously at the sight. Belinda, two spots of high colour in her pale cheeks, stretched out her hands. Jenny did the same and took a step forward. For a second she seemed enveloped in an icy mist, where her sight blurred and her senses numbed, then she was standing in that other room, shivering with cold and fear, but excited beyond belief.

Without waiting to dress herself, she ran to the leaded windows, through which drifted the scent of hay and the sounds of summer. She just *had* to see if everything was as Belinda had said it would be.

Sure enough, there was the paddock and the two horses, the grey and the brown, standing head to tail and lazily swishing away the flies. There was the old black and white sheepdog lying in the shade of the barn, and an orange kitten scampering in and out of the wide barn door. So absorbed was she that she paid no attention to a voice from below that was calling on an ever-increasing note of anger: "Belinda! Belin-dah!"

She ran back to the mirror. "Oh, Belinda, it's every bit as wonderful as you said . . ." she began, then stopped dead. The shield-shaped glass with its three little drawers stood on a dark oak table, but it did not reflect, as she had expected it to, her own cosy room. Instead, the dark outlines of the farm furniture loomed behind her and—worse—there was no sign of Belinda anywhere.

As she stood there in mounting fear and puzzlement, the dark shape of a stern-faced woman in black appeared in the doorway, crying, "Belinda, you lazy good-for-nothing! How many times have I got to call my lungs out before . . ." She stopped short in her scolding as she saw Jennifer crouching naked before the mirror. "*Now* what are you up to, you fiendish girl?" she cried, storming into the room. "What is the meaning of this wicked nakedness? Wait till I tell your Papa of *this*!"

Jennifer cringed back against the traitorous mirror. "I'm *not* Belinda," she whimpered, her heart pounding with terror, "I'm Jennifer, and I want to go home . . ."

The strange disappearance of Jennifer Vidler remains a mystery. No one—least of all the police, who were eventually called in—could explain how a girl could disappear completely from a sixth-floor flat in a large London block; particularly one who apparently was not wearing any of her clothes. At least, this was according to her distracted mother, who had been in the living-room of the flat all the time and swore her daughter never left it, clothed or unclothed.

Nor could they explain why the clothes which she had last been seen wearing were found crumpled in an untidy heap before the dressing-table, nor why there appeared to be on them the print of a small, dusty hand, while beside them was a large mound of dust, which had scattered in a fine film over everything when the door had been opened.

Perhaps the most amazing thing of all was that the mirror on the dressing-table—which, Jennifer's mother had tearfully maintained to the sceptical police, had always been kept as bright and as silver as the day it was made—was all blotched and dark, so that no reflection of any kind could be seen in it.

After a while people gave the whole thing up as an insoluble mystery, but they all said it was just too bad for poor Jennifer, wherever she had got to. How right they were!

TAKEOVER

by DAVID LANGFORD

"I'M afraid it's bad news, Garry," said Dr Clarke.

"Oh Dad! You mean we're not going to the Manor after all?" He'd been looking forward to the visit for weeks. Quern Manor! Where the ghosts were supposed to walk!

"No. I've just phoned the garage and it seems the car's not ready. Needs a part they haven't got. So we can't go. But—"

"You didn't really want to go to that nasty place," his mother said soothingly. "It's not healthy, ghosts and all that, even if you are so mad to see one. Besides, your father's arranged something else—something you'll like, and you as well, John—"

"Let me tell them, dear," Dr Clarke managed to put in. Always the same, Garry thought. Once Mum started she wouldn't stop.

John said firmly: "*I* didn't want to hunt ghosts. There's no such thing."

"Ssshh! I've rung this young fellow I know at the university—he works for me—and he's going to show you the computer there. Very interesting, I believe. We'll go to Quern some other day, Garry."

"Now doesn't that sound more fun than visiting stuffy old Quern? Anyway, if there *are* any ghosts there, they wouldn't come out on a visiting day."

"Sure, Mum. I don't mind." Garry could see that making a fuss would be absolutely useless. But just in case he seemed to be giving up too easily, he added with great emphasis: "Like Dad says, we can go to Quern *next* time it's open."

And John, when he realised that he was going to see a computer, simply shouted: "Great!"

A horn tooted merrily outside.

"That'll be him now, boys. His name's Martin Hoare, and he's a nice fellow. Don't give him any trouble."

As he spoke, Dr Clarke was heading for the door, with Garry and John behind and their mother bringing up the rear. The horn blew again; the door opened; outside in the sunshine was an extraordinarily battered Mini, and in the Mini was a pleasant-faced young man, plump and fair-haired.

"Martin, this is Garry, this is John.—This is Martin Hoare, one of the most inveterate slackers in the computer trade. He'll show you the machines that are going to take over."

"Hello," said John and Garry.

"Hello—hop in," said Martin with a grin. "Don't worry, Dr Clarke, I'll deliver them back by five. See you."

The engine gave a mighty roar, there came a sound as though something had fallen off the chassis, and the car jerked forward.

Garry decided not to be disappointed, whatever happened. The day was so hot and bright that (he admitted to himself) Quern Manor might just have been a bit boring. This wasn't the weather for ghosts at all.

They stopped outside the university computer building, a tall place that seemed to be all windows. Martin led them confidently inside. A lift took them down into the basement . . . and there was the computer. It didn't look impressive at all—simply a lot of boxes like white filing cabinets scattered over the floor of a huge, very clean room.

"They're joined together by wires under the floor," Martin said. He pointed. "That's the central processor, the 'brain' of the whole thing—those are arithmetic units—those are memory stores—" But all the boxes looked the same.

"Can we see it working?" John asked hopefully. It would be a short visit if they didn't, thought Garry.

"Come this way," said Martin. They followed him back, out of the room and into the lift, up four floors.

A short, short, visit . . . No, that was silly. "Where are we going?" Garry said. "Is there another computer?"

"No . . . Here."

It was a little room, quite empty apart from a teletype and some chairs. As in the basement, everything was spotless white. Martin arranged three chairs in front of the teletype and sat in the middle one. He beckoned, and they sat on either side of him.

"This," he said, switching the teletype on, "connects directly to the computer. There are eighty terminals like this, scattered all over the university buildings, and you can work the computer from any of them. This way we don't bother the people downstairs. Shall I make it do some sums, for a start?" He typed mysterious instructions on the teletype keyboard, and after a moment the computer typed READY.

"Oh—what's eighty-four times a hundred and fifty-three?" said John.

85*153 was what Martin typed. "We use an asterisk to mean multiplying," he explained. There was a rattle and the machine typed 13005.

"That was quick," Garry said grudgingly.

"That's nothing. I could work that out with this." Martin produced a pocket calculator, no bigger than a cigarette-packet. "But look now." His fingers played across the keyboard again, and this time, when he finished, the

91

computer drew out a noughts-and-crosses diagram:

"Want to play?" he invited.

"How?" said John.

"The top row squares are numbered 1, 2, 3; the middle ones 4, 5, 6; and so on. Just type a number . . ."

John typed 5, and the machine instantly drew out a second diagram, with an X in the centre and an 0 of its own added in the top left-hand corner.

In half a minute the game was drawn.

"Your turn," said Martin to Garry.

"No thanks. It's not much of a game."

John played again, and drew again; and again.

"What interests *you*?" Martin asked. "Not this game— but draughts maybe, or chess? The machines are taking over there, as well!"

"I'm interested in ghosts," Garry said carefully. Martin seemed taken aback.

"Well!" he said with a sudden smile. "Well!—I might have something to interest you, after all. These machines do a lot more than sums and noughts-and-crosses, you know."

John had drawn the tenth or twelfth game, and looked a little bored. "Dad says they're so stupid they don't even know the time of day."

"Just a figure of speech, that. Look—" He typed TIME. The machine responded with 15:52:31. "Three fifty-two and thirty-one seconds. How's that?"

Garry laughed, and checked his watch. (It was half a minute slow.) "But they do go wrong, don't they? You're always hearing about people getting final demands for no pounds and no pence."

"Yes . . ." Martin became a little more serious. "Look at it like this—You know your multiplication tables, of course."

"Yes!" They were both a little affronted.

"Ever get a wrong answer when you multiply?" Martin's eyes were gleaming now.

"Well, once in a while," Garry admitted. John said nothing, but looked sheepish.

"So the tables must be wrong?"

"No . . ." Garry thought hard. "You mean *people* make the mistakes."

"That's right. They type a wrong number, perhaps, and all kinds of garbage comes out—the computer doesn't know any better. But you were talking about ghosts."

He tapped the keys. They went down with faint buzzing sounds, but nothing happened.

"Curse it. I'll bet the machine is going haywire just to bust up my argument!" Martin laughed wryly, and the boys joined him. Suddenly the teletype rattled again:

TEMPORARY FAULT

FAULT CLEARED

"Thank goodness for that. Now, another thing we use computers for is storing information, and what they call data-processing. You could feed in the birth-certificates of everyone in England, and in two seconds the computer could tell you—oh—the surname of every eleven-year-old called Garry, for example."

"Why would you want to know—?" John began. Garry nudged him and he stopped.

"Now—ghosts! Ever hear of the Ghost Researchers?"

"*Yes*! I want to be one, one day." This was something Garry hadn't expected.

"Well, it just happens that they store their information in this machine. The computer sorts out reports of ghosts for them." A wink. "Strictly the files are protected so you can't get at them, but sshh! I have my ways."

He typed a rapid string of code-words, and again the teletype said READY.

"Think of a haunted house . . ."

Garry's reply was automatic: "Quern Manor."

QUERN MANOR, Martin typed. And in reply came:
QUERN MANOR, HUNTINGDONSHIRE
BUILT: 1545
REPORTED HAUNTED SINCE: 1693
REPORTED SIGHTINGS: 256
RECURRENT SIGHTINGS: 7
AUTHENTICATED GHOSTS: 5: IDENTIFICA-
TIONS FOLLOW:
1/ THIRD DUKE OF QUERN: KILLED 1632 IN
DUEL
2/ SON OF FOURTH DUKE: MURDERED BY
BRIGANDS 1705
3/ (POSS.) CHAPEL PRIEST: DIED 1780 (SUP-
POSEDLY OF FRIGHT) . . .

The information rolled out; Garry watched, fascinated. Though John seemed highly uninterested, Martin obligingly caused the machine to print full details of Garry's favourite haunted houses. One day he would visit them all . . .

"Even when it comes to ghosts," Martin said, grinning, "the machines are taking over. This better than Quern?"

"Oh, I don't know. We might have seen something there."

John said wryly, "At least now you know what you *might* have seen!"

"If you saw anything." Obviously Martin was another sceptic.

"You don't have any ghosts here?" Garry asked politely, with a faint smile. If they wanted to tease him, he'd tease right back.

Martin leant back and roared with laughter. Then he reached to the keyboard again. "Only one way to find out!"

COMP BUILDING, he typed. "It'll say NOT KNOWN, of course."

But he was wrong.

COMP BUILDING

BUILT: 1962

HAUNTED SINCE: APRIL 26 1976

"That's today," Martin whispered.

REPORTED SIGHTINGS: 0

RECURRENT SIGHTINGS: 0

AUTHENTICATED GHOSTS: 1: IDENTIFICATION FOLLOWS:

1/ UNCERTAIN

The teletype stopped and left a vast silence in the little room . . . It was hard to say why, but the bright strip-lighting and white walls suddenly seemed a little creepy. Garry laughed, nervously. What sort of ghost would walk in this place? A ghost of polished chrome?

"Somebody downstairs is playing tricks," said Martin firmly. He stood up and strode out; the children followed. Just a few seconds later, they bumped into a white-coated man whom Martin seemed to know.

"Ah, there you are," the man said. "Sorry the kids' visit was spoilt."

"Eh? How so?"

"We had a great time," Garry put in, not wanting to seem ungrateful.

"For a while, maybe, but of course the machine broke down at four . . . . Some fool repairman was checking circuits and spilt his tea in the central processor. You know, the computer's brain," he added for the boys' benefit. "Burnt out! Kaput! *Somebody's* going to catch it . . ."

"So it's dead?" John asked.

"Yes," said the man. " 'Scuse me . . . " He walked on.

"Wait a minute," said Garry, with a puzzled glance at his watch. "Four o'clock? We only just stopped, and it's nearly five."

Martin was quite silent. His lips moved once or twice, but no words came out. After a long pause, he murmured "Temporary Fault?"

A ghost of polished chrome . . . Garry shivered a little. Finally, remembering Martin's earlier joke, he said in an uncertain voice; "Even when it comes to ghosts, the machines are taking over!"

A RED, RED ROSE

by RUTH CAMERON

"My aunt Emily, your great-aunt, is a recluse," his father said, as they drove through the twisting Devonshire lanes. "That's why you've never met her. She lives all by herself in a caravan and doesn't welcome visitors."

"Then why are we visiting her?" Tom asked.

"Because she's over seventy now and she's had a spot of heart trouble, so I like to keep in touch in case she ever needs help. She'll probably send me away with a flea in my ear, but there it is. Well, we've arrived. This is Green Pool Wood."

"What a super name. Is there a green pool?"

"There is. Very pretty it is, too. You'll see it."

They left the car by the roadside and entered the wood. It was a windy summer day. The sun flickered in and out as clouds blew across its face. Birds sang and leaves rustled in the moving air. At first the path was narrow and overhung by trees, then they came to a clearing where a large pool stretched out before them. Because of the trees reflected in it, the water looked green.

"Green Pool!" said Tom. "It's fabulous!"

"It is rather out-of-this-world," his father agreed. "Now you'd better wait here. I'll go along to the caravan and see what sort of reception I get, then, if she'd like to see you, I'll come and collect you later. O.K.?"

"Fine. I'd like to wait here." He was shy and had not been looking forward to meeting a strange old woman, even if she was a relative. So his father's footsteps retreated through the rustling leaves and Tom was left alone.

It was wonderfully peaceful after the long, hot journey by car, and he felt a touch of envy for his great-aunt Emily. He wouldn't mind living here in a woodland caravan himself, close to nature, unbothered by people and school and all the practical demands of everyday life. His eyes soaked up the greenness of the pool and the trees, and the wind became still so that everything fell silent. There was an eeriness about this sudden silence. He was aware of it. As if time had stood still . . . or ceased to exist . . .

Then the silence was broken by a laugh, a sweet, young, gay laugh, mocking, feminine, and he turned his head to see a girl running through the trees towards the pool, and being pursued by a young man. They were playing some sort of game, thought Tom, and they hadn't seen him, for when the young man overtook the girl, he seized her in his arms and kissed her.

Tom drew farther back under the willow tree which sheltered him. He felt rather embarrassed. Should he betray his presence or stay hidden? He took the line of least resistance, stayed hidden, and hoped they'd soon go away. But they didn't. They sat down on the bank.

"I've got something for you," said the young man. "I hope it isn't squashed. No—it's all right." From his pocket he had brought a red rose. Solemnly he presented it to her. "A symbol of my eternal love," he said. "In the words of Robert Burns, 'My love is like a red, red rose'."

She burst out laughing. "Martin, you *are* sentimental! Queen Victoria is dead, you know. You've been reading too many Jane Austen novels, with gallant men courting fair ladies. You're a sentimental silly." Her words were mocking, but she was beautiful, Tom thought, with her mass of black hair flowing over her shoulders, her tanned skin, her big dark eyes, her long dress adding grace to her slender figure. There was mischief and wildness in her, too, a touch of the daredevil which appealed to him. It evidently appealed to this Martin person also, for he said:

She tossed the flower into the pool . . .

"I may be sentimental, but I don't care. I really do love you. You only laugh when I tell you that. How can I make you believe me? Tell me what to do to prove my love and I'll do it. Anything!"

"All right." She stood up, the red rose in her hand. She tossed the flower right out into the middle of the pool. "Now bring the red, red rose back to me," she said, "and I'll believe you."

"Oh, you devil-girl!" But he was laughing now as he peeled off his shirt, waded into the pool, then swam towards the floating rose.

The events that followed this lovers' game were shocking and terrifying. For as Martin swam closer to the flower, something seemed to hold him back, to drag him down. He fought against some invisible undertow, gave a choked cry and sank, the green water covering his head.

The girl ran to the edge of the pool. "Martin! What's happened Martin!"

His head came up once, only to sink again.

"Help!" screamed the girl. "Help! Help! Someone come! Help! Oh, God—I can't swim—I can't swim—Help! Help!"

Tom could swim, although he'd never done any lifesaving. He wanted to jump into the pool and try to rescue the drowning man, but paralysis seemed to be gripping his limbs. He literally couldn't move, although he struggled to do so. It was like a nightmare in which you're being pursued by wild beasts but can't run away. He struggled —struggled—and then felt someone shaking his shoulder, freeing his limbs by that touch . . .

"Wake up, Tom." His father was there.

A dream. It had only been a dream after all. There was, of course, no sign of the girl. The whole gruesome incident simply had not happened. Oh, the relief . . .

"We must drive into the village and fetch a doctor," his father was saying.

"Why? Is your Aunt Emily ill?" Tom asked dazedly, hurrying along beside his father.

"Yes. That is—she's dead, Tom. She must have had a heart attack. It looks to me as if she died in her sleep."

Tom said nothing. The news didn't mean much to him as he'd never even met Emily. He was more shaken by the effects of his recent dream than by the real event of the old woman's death. He told his father about the dream as they drove to the village, and when he'd finished the other said: "Tom, why are you pretending that was a dream?"

"Pretending? I'm not. When it was happening, I didn't know I was dreaming. One never does. Or almost never. I only knew it was a dream when you woke me up."

"You must have heard the story at some time, then, and it stuck in your mind. Did your mother tell you?"

"No, Dad. What story?"

"A tragedy in Aunt Emily's past. When she was seventeen she had a boy friend called Martin. He adored her, and she loved him too, in her own way, but she couldn't resist tormenting him sometimes. One summer afternoon she did throw a rose into Green Pool and tell him to fetch it for her, to prove his love. It was just a game, with a thread of feminine cruelty in it. But there are dangerous weeds in that pool which entangle swimmers' feet and pull them down. That's what happened to poor Martin. He was drowned."

"And it was her fault," murmured Tom. "She must have felt terrible. In fact, she did." He saw her anguished face again in his mind's eye.

"She did indeed," his father agreed. "She was overwhelmed by remorse. It affected her whole life. From being a flirtatious young woman, very much aware of her own attractiveness, she withdrew into herself, avoided men, never even married. She earned her living as a teacher at the village school and was respected, but was never really popular. It was as if she was afraid to give or receive

101

affection. She often walked in the wood and sat by the pool. No one could stop her. She couldn't let him go, you see . . . or perhaps he couldn't let her go. Anyway, when she retired she went to live in that caravan near Green Pool. And now she's dead, poor old thing, and all that anguish seems to be so much waste. Did you really dream that incident, Tom? You're sure you hadn't heard the story from someone?"

"Quite sure, Dad. I swear it. I saw it happen, just as if it was really happening."

"Extraordinary," murmured his father. "How little we know about life, for all our science and our book-learning."

Tom thought deeply, then said: "Perhaps things that happen are always still there really—like turning on the telly. I mean, the programme's there all the time, but you have to turn the right knob to get it. So maybe when one's asleep, one sometimes sort of turns a knob on the past, and gets the—the programme, as if it were a recording. Perhaps there are recordings of past events all round us, only we don't know where the switch is to turn them on."

"Don't get too fanciful," his father said. "We've got to be very practical now. I'll have to return to the caravan with the doctor, so we must find someone to look after you till I get back."

"Oh, no—let me stay with you. I want to. I'm not frightened. I love Green Pool Wood, in spite of the dream."

His father gave in.

They found the doctor at his house and the three of them drove back to the wood. The place was bathed in moonlight by that time and so beautiful that it seemed enchanted. They walked along the same path until they reached the pool, then the doctor suggested: "If the boy would care to wait here . . ."

"Good idea," agreed Tom's father. "You'll be all right,

won't you, Tom? Stay quietly here. We shan't be long. No falling asleep."

"No, Dad. As if I would!"

"Good boy." His father's comforting pressure on his shoulder. So real. So much more important than any dream. Then he and the doctor went on to the caravan.

Tom crossed to his special place under the willow tree and gazed at the water. Green Pool was not green now. It was silver and black. Silver for life, black for death, he thought. *Everything* is here. Past, present, future. Silver and black. And then—colour suddenly—a glow of red—for there, magically floating in the centre of the pool, was the red rose.

I'm not dreaming this time, thought Tom, although it was as if he had stepped back into his dream, picked up the thread of it from the moment of his previous waking. Yet the scene was different. No green and gold. All silver and black. The redness of the rose was the link between the dream scene and this one. The girl was standing on the shore, her face very sad. Now there was a movement in the water. The man's head appeared. He stretched out an arm and seized the rose. He set it between his teeth and swam towards the shore. When he landed, he tossed the rose to the girl, who caught it in both hands and pressed it to her heart. She was radiant now. He took her in his arms. They stood in close embrace, as if they would never let each other go again.

Tom stared and stared at these timeless lovers in the stillness and silence of this timeless time. The whole world of the night seemed to be standing still, as the lovers imprinted themselves on some eternal landscape . . .

A little wind blew up. Things began to move again. And Tom found that he was staring at the outlines of two little trees whose branches had intertwined . . .

A movement behind him. His father was there.

"We're going back now, Tom. The doctor's coming.

He'll see to everything tomorrow. She died of a heart attack, as I guessed, poor Aunt Emily. However, there are worse ways to go. At least she went peacefully, in the place which she loved and where she felt at home."

"She's all right now," Tom said, and his father accepted the statement at its face value, saying, "Yes, she's all right. Death is nothing to be afraid of. It's part of nature." There was a little silence, and he added: "Something rather odd—" He stopped.

"What, Dad?"

"A little mystery. The doctor and I were both puzzled. Someone must have gone into the caravan while we were away. A passing gipsy, perhaps."

"Why? What had happened?"

"She was lying as I'd left her, except that her face was happier—although that could be an illusion on my part. But the odd thing was that someone had placed a flower on her breast. A rose. Fresh. Fragrant. A beautiful red rose. But who put it there, or why, no one will ever know."

Except me, thought Tom. *I* know.

THE WOODSEAVES GHOSTS

by CATHERINE GLEASON

"THE only snag about staying at Woodseaves," said David Mitchell, "is the library."

"Yes," his sister Sally agreed. "Do you remember how frightened we were when we first saw it? We were sure there were ghosts about, hiding in the corners!"

"I'm not so sure that it isn't haunted," said David, with an air of mystery. Sally was two years younger than him and she usually believed every word he said.

Her eyes grew big as saucers. "You don't really think so, do you? What do you mean?"

"Well, you remember reading in that local history book about the boy and girl who were supposed to have disappeared in there? It was exactly a hunded and fifty years ago that they vanished. So they might turn up again." His voice dropped to a whisper. "One of these Fridays, when we're in the library doing our school work, the air will turn cold and the door will slowly start to open . . . cree-eak . . ."

"Oh, stop it!" cried Sally. "You're making me shiver!"

"And then," continued David in a creepy voice, "something dressed in a long white gown will glide in . . . and—grab you!"

Sally gave a little shriek and covered her ears, while David burst out laughing. "Only teasing you, silly."

"You are horrid, David," said Sally, giggling in spite of herself. "You're just trying to scare me because we have to do some work in there tonight. Well, I'm not afraid!"

"Neither am I, really," said David. "Come on, slow-coach, we're going to be late for tea. Where's Max?"

The heavy golden labrador lumbered up to them and they made their way back through Woodseaves Park to the Hall.

Great-Uncle Timothy Mitchell owned the Hall, and lived there with his housekeeper Martha and, of course, Max. Like his house, Uncle Tim was rather Victorian and rambling, but David and Sally were very fond of him and loved spending their summer holidays at Woodseaves.

This was the first year their parents hadn't been with them, because their father had taken a job in America that summer and Mrs. Mitchell had gone with him.

Martha was very neat and motherly and precise, and she had been Uncle Tim's housekeeper for donkeys' years. She was only ever strict about one thing, and that was their doing an hour or so's work in the library on the subjects they hadn't done very well in at school. This, as David said, was the one snag about staying there, but then it wasn't much of a disadvantage, considering all the other things that Woodseaves had to offer. Midway between the town and the country, everything was within easy reach, from riding stables to a cinema.

"What did you do with yourselves today, children?" Uncle Tim asked them over tea.

He and Martha had always called David and Sally "children", and David suspected that they always would, no matter how big they grew.

"We fed the goldfish in the pond, and then David climbed a tree and nearly fell in the stream, and then the Smithson twins took us over to South Meadow to see the lambs," said Sally. "They're getting quite big now."

"What, the Smithsons?" The old man looked startled.

"No, Uncle, the lambs," giggled Sally. Uncle Tim was so vague at times.

"I was reading about ghosts in a local history book," said David. "Do you know there are supposed to be two of them here at Woodseaves?"

"That's right." Uncle Tim chuckled. "A brother and his young sister, about the same ages as you two. They were said to have been murdered by their wicked stepmother, or some such nonsense."

"Why?" demanded Sally, who had more than her fair share of curiosity.

"The stepmother wanted Woodseaves for her own sons, and the other two were in the way, I suppose."

"Really, Mr Timothy, you shouldn't be filling the children's heads with such stories," said Martha reprovingly. "We've lived here more years than we care to remember, and we've never seen any ghosts."

"That's probably because there aren't any such things," suggested David.

"Exactly. Ghosts don't exist."

Sally wasn't so sure.

"There. Finished at last." David threw down his pen thankfully and stretched, pushing back his chair. It had taken him nearly an hour to plough through his French exercise.

"Well, hang on a minute," said Sally crossly. She was struggling with a maths problem.

"O.K." Idly, David glanced around the library. All the other rooms at Woodseaves were light and modern-furnished, but even in the height of summer the library looked gloomy, damp and ancient. Hundreds of old books, some very valuable, were shut into dark, glass-fronted cases against the walls, and the firelight cast weird dancing reflections on to them.

"Nearly finished now," said Sally, one hand stroking Max, who shifted restlessly beside her. The big dog always seemed uneasy in the library. Suddenly he jumped up and ran over to the window, barking furiously.

"Max! Come and lie down," ordered David.

Max slunk reluctantly away from the window, tail down, to the opposite corner of the room. He made a funny sort of noise, half way between a whine and a howl, and scratched at the door, looking back at them with piteous eyes. David opened the door for him and the dog shot out of the room as if something was after him.

"That's strange," said Sally. "Maybe he saw a cat outside?"

"I don't think so." David peered out of the window at the dusky night. "Perhaps he—"

Suddenly all the lights went out, and, except for the glowing fire, the room was plunged into darkness. Sally gave a little scream.

"It's all right," said David calmly, sitting by the fire. "The lights have fused, that's all. I expect Uncle will have them on again in a minute."

"I hope so," said Sally. "It's rather scary in here with —oh!" She broke off with a cry of astonishment.

David swung round and followed her gaze to the window. His mouth dropped open in sheer amazement as he saw two strange figures, hand in hand, passing straight through the window into the library!

David and Sally clutched each other in terror. But the figures did not look terrifying; they were a boy and a girl, dressed in old-fashioned clothes.

"Do not be afraid. We are not come to harm you," said the boy.

"What . . . who are you?" asked David in a quavery voice.

"My name is Lucretia, and this is my brother, Comus," said the girl, with a slight bow.

"Er . . . how do you do," said Sally, a little unsteadily.

"May we sit down? We have been wandering for many

years, and we are somewhat fatigued," the boy introduced as Comus said politely.

Sally rubbed her eyes and stared. The ghostly figures sat quite calmly in the two leather armchairs opposite and, through their outlines, she could see the chairs quite clearly.

"David," she whispered, "do you think we're dreaming?"

"No," said David excitedly. "I think they're the two who were murdered here—don't you remember Uncle Tim's story?—and they've come back to the—to the scene of the crime," he finished lamely.

"Indeed, you are right," said Lucretia in her sweet, light voice. "Our lives were cut short very much against our wills, one hundred and fifty years ago this very evening."

David nodded. "Uncle Tim told us about you."

Sally wriggled in her chair. Half of her was scared enough to dash straight out of the library, shrieking for Uncle Tim, but the other half was full of inquisitiveness. After a short struggle, curiosity won.

"How did it happen?" she asked finally. "Your being murdered, I mean."

"Yes, how?" David, too, was still a little frightened, and spoke rather more aggressively than he intended. "Our uncle said you were killed by a wicked stepmother, like people in a fairy tale, and it all sounds very fishy to me."

Comus and Lucretia looked at each other in a puzzled way.

"It had nothing to do with fish," said Comus. "It was poisoned veal, as I remember."

"That is right," said Lucretia. "You see, our mama died when we were a little younger than you are now, and Papa married again, almost straight away. He was a very good man, and he wished to secure a second mother for us."

"But his second wife, our stepmother, was a most wicked woman," continued Comus. "She was widowed too, and she married Papa in order to provide for her own baby sons. Really, you know, she did not care a rap for him or for us. She only wanted her children to have Woodseaves, and we stood in the way, because Woodseaves would have been ours when we were old enough to inherit it."

"At first, we did not realise the extent of her malice," Lucretia resumed, "though we did consider it odd when she told us that deadly nightshade was good for us, and to eat as much as we could if ever we found it growing wild."

"And she was always suggesting that we go for a bathe in the deepest part of the river," added Comus. "After we told her repeatedly that we could not swim!"

"Yet she was always very pleasant to us," Lucretia sighed. "We hardly believed she could wish us any harm. Then, one evening, she served us a dish of veal here in the library where we were reading, and that was that."

"You were poisoned?" asked Sally, round-eyed.

"Yes—we fell asleep, and awoke like this." Comus held up a transparent hand.

"And what happened to your stepmother?" asked David.

"She died of the consumption shortly afterwards, and confessed on her deathbed to having poisoned us. Her sons did not long survive her, and so it was all a wasted effort, really." Lucretia looked sadly into the fire.

"What a shame!" cried the warm-hearted Sally indignantly. "I think it's terrible that you should have had such short, unhappy lives. Honestly, David, we don't know how lucky we are, do we?"

"You're right," agreed David seriously. "We do have marvellous parents, when you come to think about it. None of this wicked-stepmother stuff at all."

Comus and Lucretia exchanged glances of something like envy.

"Your parents, then, are very kind?" asked Comus wistfully.

"Oh, yes! They couldn't be nicer," said Sally eagerly. "I wish we could help you," she added to their phantom visitors.

"Perhaps you can," said Comus at once. "For we have come here tonight to offer you a proposition."

"What kind of proposition?" David asked suspiciously.

"We wish to change places with you," said Comus simply. "If you are agreeable to our suggestion, we would become you, and you would become——"

"Ghosts?" said Sally faintly.

"Er . . . I don't think we'd like that very much, thank you," said David. "Anyway, why us?"

"Why, because you are here at Woodseaves," said Lucretia. "And you are about the same ages as we are. Being a ghost can be great fun, you know," she added mischievously. "Watch me!"

And before their eyes, she vanished. David and Sally watched breathlessly as a heavy vase rose into the air, apparently by itself, and flew across the room. "Catch!" came a gleeful cry from nowhere, and David had to go into a quick rugby dive to save the vase before it hit the ground.

There was a tinkling laugh and Lucretia appeared again. "There! You see? Some very naughty ghosts do that sort of thing all the time."

"I don't think we'd want to drift about chucking vases around, actually," said Sally, as David rubbed his bruised elbows.

"Oh, dear!" sighed Lucretia.

"Perhaps you would prefer to reside in the celestial regions?" suggested Comus.

111

"What do you mean?" asked Sally. "You do talk oddly, you know!"

"Everybody talked like that hundred and fifty years ago," David reminded her.

"Precisely. I beg your pardon," Comus apologised to Sally. "I meant to say, how about Heaven?"

And just then, the door opened.

"Are you still in here, children?" Martha fiddled with the light switch. "Have both of the light bulbs gone? What a nuisance!" She came into the firelit room, glancing straight at the ghostly figures in the armchairs.

"We were just talking, Martha," said Sally.

"Well, don't stay too long, dears. Bed in half an hour, you know."

"Why didn't Martha see you?" asked David, as soon as she had gone.

"We did not wish her to," said Comus.

"What was that you said about Heaven?" Sally demanded impatiently.

"My brother wondered if you would care to go there," said Lucretia carelessly.

"Have you really been to Heaven? I don't believe it!" said David.

"Indeed we have," said Lucretia, with indignation. "We might have stayed there, too, but that we kept on hankering after life on earth, and THEY do not like it if you are half-hearted about Heaven. And so we came back. Won't you change places with us, please?" she asked imploringly. "THEY wouldn't mind, you know."

David and Sally did not ask who THEY were; they rather thought they knew already.

"Well, really, I don't think . . . " began David doubtfully, but Sally was overcome with curiosity and cut in with:

"What's it really like in Heaven? Do tell us all about it."

"Oh, it is a wonderful place, of course, but much depends on whereabouts you go. There are many different sections," explained Comus.

"How do you mean?" Sally was puzzled. Heaven was Heaven, wasn't it?

"Well," said Lucretia, "there is one part where all the soldiers go who have been killed in battle. They feast and drink all the time, and have their wounds bandaged. I found it monotonous—dull, you know," she added, wrinkling her nose and tossing back her light brown ringlets. "All of their conversation concerns war and battles. It is messy too, with all that blood and iodine."

"Valhalla!" cried David excitedly. "I've heard about that at school—it's the Heaven of the Vikings. Do all the Chinese Kung Fu fighters who get beaten go there as well?"

Comus looked puzzled. "I have never heard of this Kung Fu," he confessed. "The Eastern people generally seem to go to Nirvana, where they do nothing but sit and think all the time. They call it meditation. Now that really is dull."

"The Mount Olympus one is quite pleasant," said Lucretia doubtfully. "If you like hatching plots and chasing fauns through forests, that is. I believe they have a few unicorns and winged horses there, too."

"Really? Winged horses?" Sally was thrilled. She was pony-mad.

"Yes. And there is ordinary Heaven as well, where you walk on clouds and wear haloes," said Comus. "A great many Royal Air Force pilots seem to end up there. I think they really mean to go to Valhalla, but they cannot resist the wings, you see."

"It also helps if you play a musical instrument," added Lucretia. "Won't you change places with us? I am sure you would like it very much."

"How could you do that?" asked David curiously.

113

"Oh! That is very simple," said Comus. "We hold your hands for a second, and concentrate very hard, and our minds would change places with yours. You see? It is extremely easy."

"Well—I'm really very sorry," said David, "but I'm afraid we can't."

"No," said Sally regretfully. "It's our parents, you see. They would miss us terribly."

"Ah, but they would never know," argued Comus. "After all, we would look exactly the same as you. It's just that we should have swapped minds. Within a few weeks we could learn to talk as you do, and then nobody at all would be able to tell the difference."

"I'm afraid it's impossible," said David slowly.

There was a sad little pause. Comus looked very downcast, and Lucretia dabbed her eyes with a transparent lace handkerchief. Sally thought longingly about unicorns and winged horses, and David tried very hard not to think of Valhalla.

"Well!" Comus said finally. "Then there is nothing more to be said. We had better be going."

"I'm so sorry we couldn't help," said Sally, "and it's been simply marvellous talking to you."

"It has been our pleasure," said Comus and Lucretia politely. "We wish you goodnight." And they put out their hands in farewell.

"Goodbye," said Sally and David, and without thinking they shook hands with the ghostly pair.

"Now then, children!" Martha pushed open the library door. "It really is getting late. Oh, good, the lights are working again. I've cooked you some fish fingers for a suppertime snack—come along to the kitchen before they get cold." And she bustled out again.

They looked at each other and smiled.

114

"What on earth can fishes' fingers look like, Sister? Evidently a new variety of fish has been discovered."

"Indeed; when we were here last, fish did not even have hands, let alone fingers. Let us go and try them!"

Hand in hand, they walked out of the library to find the kitchen.

THE HAUNTED RIVER

by CHARLES THORNTON

BRIAN'S father was checking his new fishing rod and talking to his wife at the same time.

"There's no reason at all why the lad can't come night fishing with me now—after all, he *is* twelve years old. Besides, if I refuse him any longer he'll begin to doubt me and start thinking I'm a burglar."

Brian looked at his mother pleadingly.

"Well," she said, "all right then. At least it's the school holidays, so he'll be able to sleep all day tomorrow." She turned to Brian. "But no running off on your own. Stay with your father. You will keep an eye on him, won't you, John?"

"Stop worrying," said his father, kissing her cheek. "Come on, son—let's get the packing finished."

Brian bristled with excitement, and he was not sure whether it was over the prospect of catching fish or the fact that it was night time. He had never stayed up all night before.

As the train rattled through the countryside, Brian reminded his father about the weather forecast.

"They said it might rain tonight, Dad—hope it won't stop you fishing."

His father laughed.

"Good lord—you've got a lot to learn, I can see that. Some of the finest fish are caught in the rain. In any case, I've got the oilskins packed."

It was quite a walk to the river from the station, and it was already very dark. Heavy clouds partly obscured the moon, causing long shadows of the trees and branches to sway in the night breeze. Brian clung closely to his father, and then they felt the first rain. It lashed into their faces as the wind carried it diagonally, and they paused briefly to drag on the oilskins. Brian at last could hear the river lapping at the bank and felt a surge of excitement as its silver gleam came into view.

"This spot will do," said his father, sorting through some bait. "You watch me, then you can find your own spot further along. What about a competition, eh?"

The prospect of perhaps catching more fish than his father appealed to Brian very much, but after fifteen minutes of waiting and watching the line he began to feel restless. Learning very quickly that conversation disturbed the fish, and as his father sat hunched with bowed head in the ever-increasing rain, he thought the time was ripe for that competition. Without a word, Brian silently eased the spare rod from its case, took a small bag of bait and stealthily crept away.

He walked about half a mile along the bank before deciding to stop. Remembering what he had been told, he soon had the line cast into the river, and, settling the rod firmly on a mound of earth, he sat down to wait for his first catch. He could just see the tip of the rod as it quivered over the water, and then the sky seemed to open. The rain gushed in torrents and hissed as it flooded the earth all around him, and he could see his rod being swept away as the mound of earth supporting it became just a small splatter of mud.

Panicking, Brian forgot his own safety. With a full-length dive he stretched his arms out into the water, but he could only touch the end of the rod with his fingertips. It drifted further away. Now he could feel the current pull-

117

ing him, and the oilskins weighing him down. He fought
with all his strength, pushing down at the water, keeping
his head high, and then, through half-closed eyes, he saw
the boat. It seemed to have risen from the bed of the river.
Someone was pulling strongly on two large oars, and the
craft was coming towards him.

Brian, now almost drained of strength, pushed arms and
legs to meet it, but as he got nearer the oars stopped and
a figure leaned out over the side. It appeared to hang
there, waiting for Brian to reach it. The space between
them lessened, and then Brian caught sight of its face. It
was a grinning skull, beckoning him to come. A long,
bony arm extended from a shroud-covered body, and,
from a claw-like hand, a large net drooped, waiting to
snatch him from the river. Then he remembered no more.

Dawn had already broken before Brian had sufficiently
recovered to hear how he had been pulled from the river.
He was lying cosy and warm in a bed at the local hospital.
His father and the friendly face of a policeman looked
down upon him.

"Wh . . . What happened?" stammered Brian.

"Perhaps your father had better tell you," said the
policeman.

"You nearly drowned, that's what happened, and if I
hadn't got there when I did—you would have done.
Luckily, I'd noticed the other rod was missing, or I
wouldn't have known. Anyway, I saw you in trouble and
pulled you out. We can thank this constable, who was
patrolling at the time, for getting an ambulance."

"Sorry about the rod, Dad," said Brian.

"We won't worry about that now. All I want to know
is, why didn't you strike for the bank? Why were you
making for the middle of the river?"

Brian began to relate the story of the boat and the horrible figure that had appeared to want to save him. When

he had finished, the policeman scratched his chin thought-fully.

"I doubt whether he wanted to save you, lad," he said. "More likely—push you under."

Brian's father glanced at the policeman.

"What do you mean, Constable?"

"Well, sir, this may sound very strange indeed—and a bit creepy, if I may say so—but many years ago all this land, including the river, was owned by a very greedy and ruthless baron. He wouldn't allow the local people to hunt on his land—or, indeed, fish in his river—"

Brian's father interrupted him.

"You're not going to tell me . . ."

"Just let me finish, sir, and then you can draw your own conclusions. As I was saying, he allowed them no food from the land or fish from the river. But the folks who lived hereabouts in those days were starving, so they took their chances. Those that were caught were put to death on the Baron's orders. He also had a small boat, sir, and he'd patrol the river to catch poaching fishermen—and kill them on the spot."

Brian's eyes were wide open as he listened intently to the policeman's story. Then he said: "How could he kill a poacher on the bank when he was in a boat on the river?"

"Simple, lad. He had a net. You saw it, didn't you?"

"You mean . . ."

"Exactly. The story goes that he was quite an expert with that net, and he would drift as near as possible without being seen. Then in a flash he would flick the net over the man's head and drag him through the water until he drowned."

"Awful," said Brian.

"Ah," the policeman continued, "but the people had their revenge."

"In what way?" asked Brian's father.

119

"They punctured the bottom of his boat one stormy night, and he went down in the middle of the river—quite near where you saved your son. By the way, sir, I take it you saw nothing?"

"Not a thing, Constable."

"Then we must assume from Brian that the old baron still haunts the river."

Brian's father smiled grimly.

"Can't wait to tell his mother about all this. I phoned her earlier, Brian, and she's on her way."

Brian cringed at the thought of what his mother would say, but his father gave him a broad wink.

"Don't worry," he said. "She loves ghost stories."

TIME AFTER TIME

by MARY DANBY

IT'S a strange story, and you may well not believe it. But
I shan't mind. You see, there is one person who will understand every word. One day.

It began when Papa died and we had to leave our lodg-
ings in Wembley and take a train to Dorset, where Mama
had secured a post as housekeeper to Sir William and
Lady Penderby.

I remember how grand I felt when the chauffeur came
to fetch us at the station. He let me sit at the back of the
motor-car, in the dickey, while Mama took the front pas-
senger seat. In her new velvet hat with its cockade of
pheasant feathers she looked quite the lady. The chauffeur's
name was Mr George Smith, but, as a special favour, I
was to be allowed to call him Mr George.

The sky, dark all day with rain clouds, began to clear as
we approached Sandings Manor, and I could see that it was
long and low, with square turrets at either end. It looked
somehow familiar, and I had this odd feeling that I already
knew every brick and chimney, every sill and lintel.

"Is it very old?" I asked Mr George as he drove into a
yard at the back of the house.

He switched off the engine and jumped down on to the
cobbles. "Built for the first baronet, Sir Giles Penderby,"
he told me. "Round about the time of Queen Elizabeth."
He didn't call her "Elizabeth the First", of course, because in those days there had only been one Elizabeth on
the throne of England.

121

He helped me down from the dickey, and I stood with Mama, gazing up at the windows of our new home. We would be living in the servants' quarters, but I pretended for a moment that I was a rich lady, about to take tea in the drawing-room with Lady Penderby. A rich lady, however, would not have used the kitchen entrance, as we did.

From that first day, I felt at home at Sandings. Mama, of course, was not an ordinary servant, like the kitchen-maid or the boot-boy. She and the butler, Mr Armitage, had their own sitting-room, and Mama and I shared a bedroom that was hung with pretty wallpaper and had a large rug on the floor. We were really very lucky.

I hardly ever saw the Penderbys, except from a distance. Each day, Mr George drove Sir William around his estate —he owned a great deal of farmland—and Lady Penderby wrote letters in the morning-room or made up dinner menus for the cook. Sometimes she sent for Mama, and they talked for ages about bed-linen and dressmaking and things of that sort. The third member of the family was the Penderby's son, Edward, but he was just a baby then and we only saw him when the nurse pushed his pram around the garden.

One day, when Sir William was out in the motor-car, and Lady Penderby was with Mama, somewhere upstairs, I stole out of the kitchen quarters and opened the heavy door that led to the main part of the house. This door was covered with a thick green baize, so that the servants' noise couldn't be heard by the gentry. It swung to behind me, and closed with a soft thud.

Everything was so big, so spacious. Across the hall, the great oak staircase curved past gold-framed oil paintings to the first floor, and in front of me, on a circular table, sat a silver bowl full of the sweet peas the under-gardener had picked that morning. Their scent was clean and heady, mingling richly with the smell of beeswax furniture polish.

I moved around the table, running my finger over its deeply gleaming surface, then wiped it quickly with the hem of my pinafore in case I had left any marks.

There were a great many portraits hanging on the panelled walls, but I had no difficulty in choosing the one I liked best. It showed a fine, beautiful young lady holding a black-and-white puppy, which nestled against her shoulder and looked as if it was about to lick her ear. On a small gold plate attached to the frame I read: "MISS KATE PENDERBY, WITH HER DOG FERN. T. ROGERS PINXIT, 1743." Some years later, the schoolteacher told me that "pinxit" was Latin for "he painted", and that T. Rogers was therefore the artist, but at the time I must confess I thought it was part of his name. And as most of the pictures said, "Something-or-other Pinxit," I concluded that the Pinxits must have been a very artistic family!

But I am wandering from the point. I must tell you the rest of the story before I go. And there is not much time left, now.

I was standing by the door to the drawing-room when I heard voices on the stairs. It was my mother and her ladyship. If they were to find me there, the wrong side of the baize door, I would surely be severely punished. It was too late for me to cross the hall, so, hardly pausing to think, I opened the drawing-room door and slid inside.

And that was when I saw her. She wore a green satin gown with a lace collar and cuffs, and she was sitting on the window-seat with her back to the light, so I couldn't at first see her face. By her side was a younger girl, about sixteen years old, who was working at a tapestry frame, and at their feet a puppy played with a reel of silk.

For a moment I was cold with fear, and wanted to run. Then something told me I need not be afraid, for the two on the window-seat were not aware of my presence in the room. It was as though—how can I put it?—as though I

123

were watching them on a television screen. Mind you, we had no television in those days, nor even radio—but I can remember feeling a kind of remoteness.

They were chattering eagerly about something, and I moved closer so that I could hear what they were saying. As I did so, I recognised the lady in green. Of course. It was Kate Penderby, the young lady I had so admired in the painting.

Her voice was light and high, and she said: "But my dear Anne, it is truly so. Sometimes there is half-remembered music in my head, a lute playing softly, and I have —oh no, I beg you, do not laugh—I have felt a stiff collar about my neck." She raised her hands to her throat and indicated an area as might have been occupied by a ruff in earlier times.

Anne smiled. "Kate, your fancies are too much for me. Next you will be telling me you see rushes strewn about the floor!"

"Not rushes, no, but . . . oh, I swear by God's truth this is no lie, Anne. You know the terrace to the west side of this house? It was laid by my father about ten years ago. But sometimes, when I walk across it, the ground is soft beneath my feet. Not paving stones, but grass! How would you explain that? I tell you, we do not live our lives once only. We have many, many lives. Perhaps we cannot always recall our previous existences, but to say you do not remember something does not mean it never happened. I am convinced that I was here before, nearly two hundred years ago. I was a lady of the Queen's court, I believe. My name was Margaret Carnforth. You can see my grave in the local churchyard, if you've a mind to look. I know I am she, for her presence is so strong to me there that I can reach out and feel the wood of her coffin like a wall before my face. As I was born when she was born, so I died when she died."

"And Fern, too?" said Anne, laughing. "What was

"Go on, off with you!"

he last time? A Tudor dog, perhaps, sitting beneath a table to catch bones? Or was he something else? A wolf? A tame monkey? Oh, for shame, Kate!"

The other girl spoke softly now. "One day," she said thoughtfully, "I will return to Sandings. For I believe the key to it all is this house. There is something here that draws me, and I will come back."

"And will you know you were once Kate Penderby?" asked Anne mockingly. "Will you feel the lace at your throat and see poor Fern here when he has long since become a jungle elephant? Will you walk in the woods and see tiny saplings where oaks grow taller than the house? How will you remember?"

Kate gave a gentle smile. "I'll know," she said. "Somehow I'll know."

At that moment the door opened and the housemaid—Polly, I think her name was—came in with her dusters and brooms.

"My!" she exclaimed. "Whatever are you doing in here? Get back to the kitchen quick as salt before her ladyship catches you. Anyone would think you owned the place, to see you taking such liberties. Go on, off with you! You know you're not allowed Upstairs."

Of course, we weren't really upstairs, but that was what we called the Penderby's part of the house. We were Below Stairs, which meant the other side of the green baize door.

I'm wandering again, aren't I? You must forgive me. You'll find when you get to my age it can be hard to concentrate. I expect you're waiting to hear what happened to Kate, Anne and Fern. Well, I didn't even have to turn back to the window-seat to know they were no longer there. They had acted their parts, and now they had left the stage. And you know, I never did see them again. But the message was fixed in my mind, and I'm telling you now, in case *she*, the next one, is listening—as I was.

And that's the story—or most of it. During the Great

War, we stayed on at Sandings, and when my mother died I took her place as housekeeper. After the second war there were not many servants left, but I used to cook and clean for Master Edward— *Sir* Edward as he is now— and they gave me this little cottage in the grounds so that I could end my days in comfort.

Now I don't know whether or not you believe in rein-carnation, as they call it—the reappearance of a soul in another body—but I can tell you that Kate is here, as I am here, and will be again one day in the future. So many exciting things for us. Perhaps we will travel in space next time. Or live in houses under the sea. So many new things.

Oh, I'm tired now. This life has been so full. So very tired. But, please—there is no need to upset yourself. I have died before. *We* have died before. Haven't we, Kate.

Mourners at the old lady's funeral noticed fresh flowers on two other, much older graves: on the grave of Kather-ine Penderby, 1724-1786, and on one whose carving was barely readable, but the first name seemed to be Mar-garet, and the date of death 1599.

"Who could have put them there?" they asked each other, nodding their black hats together beneath the churchyard yew tree.

The verger said he had seen the old lady herself, a few days before she died, tending the graves as lovingly as she would those of dear departed friends. "But she was dazed in her mind towards the end," he added. "Talked to her-self a lot. Kept telling me about some dog. Fern, she called him. Even used to stroke him, only of course he wasn't there. Not one whisker of him. Ah well, but we all go in our own way, don't we. In our own time."

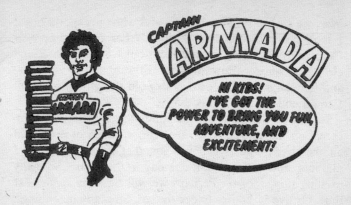

HI KIDS!
I'VE GOT THE
POWER TO BRING YOU FUN,
ADVENTURE, AND
EXCITEMENT!

Armadas are chosen by children all over the world. They're designed to fit your pocket, and your pocket money too – and they make terrific presents for friends. They're colourful, exciting, and there are hundreds of titles to choose from – thrilling mysteries, spooky ghost stories, hilarious joke books, brain-teasing quizzes and puzzles, fascinating hobby books, stories about ponies and schools – and many, many more. Armada has something for everyone.

Book Tokens

Give them
the pleasure of choosing

Book Tokens can be bought
and exchanged at most
bookshops.

Armada